The OVERKILLING THE PAST trilogy is available now

BOOK 1

Overkilling the Past

BOOK 2

WHAT COMES AROUND The Story of Karma

BOOK 3

Detective Lucas: End of an Error

ISBN: 979-8-9926441-0-4

E-Book: 979-8-9926441-1-1

Leeash35@yahoo.com

Printed in the United States · 700 Walnut Ridge Drive·

Irving, Texas 75038

This is a work of fiction. Any character that resembles any person, living or dead, is purely coincidental. So basically, even though some of these characters are named after my friends, they are nothing like them in real life. This book is dedicated to my friends at the water plant.

"YOU LOOKED!"

WILLIAM L. ASH

OVERKILLING THE PAST

When playing with death, remember, it only has to win once. You have to win every time.

Chapter 1: Introduction

I have to admit, sometimes my brain amazes me. I mean, the way it can see, assess, and then react to any situation, instantly, is incredible. It's my gift. I just know things. My intuition is fantastic. My perception is 20/20. My understanding of human nature is uncanny. It's almost as if real life moves in slow motion.

It was a typical Wednesday morning. I woke up at 4 am, showered, then drove a half hour to work, making sure I would be there to clock in at 5. I always tried to have enough buffer time, should a road be closed, or an accident cause a detour somewhere on my route.

I was exactly 2.3 miles from my job when I took a right off the freeway and saw a black Camaro pulled to the side of the road.

A woman, obviously upset, had just gotten out on the passenger side and slammed the door. She wore the same type of uniform that I had on.

It was my coworker, a woman named Carla. We'd worked together for years. I heard her yell at the driver, her husband John, then turn and start to walk up the hill towards our job.

John sped off, leaving his wife on her own.

My brain took over, I leapt into action.

"Miss Carla! Hey, Miss Carla... You trying to get a workout in? Haha," I pulled up beside her. "You're gonna be late! Get in." She did.

I didn't ask what happened, it didn't matter. I could see her eye already starting to swell. I shifted into drive and started to pull off.

Beep beep beep!

The Camaro had come around and was now behind me.

"HEY! HEY, CARLA!" John yelled.

I stopped, and without a word, I got out, nonchalantly grabbing the pistol I had sitting in the driver's door side pocket. I tucked it in the small of my back as I approached the car.

"Hey man," I said, "I'm just giving her a ride." I had my hands up as I shut my door and walked towards him. "We're gonna be late if we don't leave now. You remember me, right? Charles... Charles Brown. We met at the Christmas party." I was standing by his window.

"Yeah, what up, man? She's tripping, man. I'm telling you, that bitch tripping!"

I flinched at his choice of words.

He started to open the door to get out, but I was leaning on it, holding it closed. I grabbed my pistol.

POP! POP!

I shot him twice. One in the temple, one in the chest. The second was literally overkill since the entire right side of his face was already spread across the interior of his car.

I reached in and pressed the hazard light button, then calmly walked back to my truck.

Carla had been trying to get out. If she didn't see what I did, she heard it, and since I had the child locks set on the doors, I knew she wasn't going anywhere.

I stole the child lock idea from one of those serial killer documentaries that women seem to love. I don't see the attraction, but I do appreciate the play-by-play. Those shows are like tutorials. They offer so many tips and tricks... how-tos on how not to get caught.

I sat down in the driver's seat and pressed the barrel of my gun to her head.

"Call in sick," I demanded.

"What? Charles. What the fuck?"

I flinched, then hit her with the butt of the pistol.

"OW! FUCK!"

"LANGUAGE!" I hit her again. "Call in."

She picked up her phone to call work to say she wasn't feeling well and wouldn't make it in.

I drove down the road our building was on with the gun's barrel pressed against her cheek. I called in too, saying I'd be late due to car issues.

It was still dark, but I could see the confusion and fear on her face from the headlights of oncoming traffic.

I was giddy inside. Impressed by my brain's ability to see what was going on with Carla's domestic issue, then being able to use it to my advantage. I was an opportunist, simply playing the hand I was dealt.

Ironically, it felt like she was a gift from God, because when she first got out of the Camaro, they were stopped in front of a church.

"Does he hurt you?" I asked.

She didn't answer until I raised the pistol like I was going to hit her again.

She ducked instinctively, then nodded. I felt bad for her. Nobody should have to live in fear like that. No one should have to live their life afraid of the person who was supposed to love and protect them. Especially women and children. It made me sad as I sat and thought about it.

I was going to fix that. John wouldn't hurt her anymore. Nobody would, because Carla was going to die and I was going to be her killer.

Chapter 2: Baptism

We drove 15 minutes north in complete silence, towards a spot in the woods near a lake I like to fish at. I pulled off the road and headed down a trail after shutting off the lights. Carla never asked where we were going.

I parked where the trail ended and shut off my car.

"This is it, the end of the line. This is where you die," I said.

I got out and walked around to her side, then pulled her violently by the hair out of the vehicle.

"Put your hands out," I demanded.

"Huh? I don't under…"

I grabbed her arm and slammed a handcuff on her right wrist, then did the same to the left. I clipped a dog leash to them and started to walk, leading her like an animal, deeper into the woods.

"Charles," she said, finally offering some resistance, "why are you doing this? You don't have to do this."

I tugged hard on the dog leash, causing her to trip and fall.

"Get up!" I demanded.

"Charles…" she said, struggling to stand, "you don't have to…"

"I know I don't have to. I want to."

I tugged on the leash again, pulling her along behind me.

"Are you religious, Carla?" I asked.

"Yes."

"Which denomination?"

"Christian."

"So you pray?"

"Yes. I've been praying this whole time," she said confidently.

"To who?" I stopped at the edge of a beach, the water barely touching my boots.

"To who?" I asked again, "Jesus? You pray to Jesus, that's your God?"

"Yes."

"And you've been baptized?"

"I have, yes, but Charles, like, where is this going? What are…?"

I jumped at her, knocking her down, then, grabbing her head and neck, I dragged her into the water.

"So now that you know that you're about to die, would you call on a different God if you knew that it would save you?" I growled.

"No," she answered again, confidently.

I dunked her head in the water. This was her new baptism. I pulled her head up, giving her a chance to breathe.

"Call on Muhammad, and I will let you go," I said.

"No."

I dunked her head back down. She struggled but couldn't match my strength. She was getting weaker. I pulled her head up.

"Call on Abraham, and I will let you go."

"No. You're not going to get me to change, Charles. I'm not afraid, I'm a child of God. If you're gonna kill me, just do it," she said defiantly.

"Don't tell me what to do!" I said angrily. I pushed her head down again, this time mashing her face into the sand and gravel under the water. She was dying, I pulled her up.

"Charles, how long have I known you? This isn't you. Why are you doing this? We've been friends a long time. Stop this. Let me go, I won't tell anyone, I promise." She struggled to speak between breaths.

"How can you love a god that would allow this to happen to you?" I asked, finally releasing her and crawling back to land. I was honestly curious.

She sat up and caught her breath. Still kneeling in the water, she began to speak about her religion and her love of the church and everything it represented. I listened. Not having a religious bone in my body, I was actually a bit envious of her faith. She spoke about God as if he were real. She told me everything... all the lessons and teachings she could remember. She said she'd be willing to work with me and help try to heal whatever was hurting me so bad that it was making me do what I was doing. She answered some of the questions that nobody else had ever been able to answer in a way that made sense to me. She spoke with so much enthusiasm and with such conviction that it was hard for me not to be drawn in. Her passion for me to accept Jesus as my Lord and Savior was pure. She swore that it was the only path to heaven, and I would be forgiven for my sins. There was a glow about her, sitting there soaking wet, speaking about the glory of God... she almost had me believing.

I began to feel bad about what I was doing. Surely, a woman like her would keep her promise not to tell, right? I stood, walked over, and helped her up, then unlocked her handcuffs. It was light enough outside now that I could look her in the eyes, but I didn't. I was too ashamed of myself.

"Come on, I'll give you a ride back," I said.

"No, I'll call my sister, she'll come. You go on, go home, rest. You look so tired, Charles." She felt around her pockets for her phone.

"It's still in the car," I said, as I started to jog back to retrieve it. "I'll get it."

"Wait!" she called out. I stopped. "Why did you hit me? In the car, why did you have to hit me?"

The question froze me. I didn't have an answer, I was embarrassed. I was absolutely and completely ashamed of myself for what I did to this woman of faith. This woman that I had just nearly drowned. This woman who had just seen her husband murdered. I turned and jogged a remorseful jog back towards the truck.

"Dang it!" That's when it hit me. I turned around and ran back to where Miss Carla was standing, facing away from me, looking at the water.

POP! POP!

I shot her twice. Once in the back of her head, the other in her back. And just like her husband, the second shot was overkill.

I stood and watched to see if a soul would leave her body and float to the sky. It didn't. I left her where she fell and walked back to my truck.

My brain is so silly sometimes, I thought. There's no way in heck that I'd make it to heaven, and giving that woman hope that I was going to let her live was just cruel and unnecessary.

"You're such a butthole," I said, laughing into the rearview mirror.

I drove to Walmart to buy a new pair of Dickies and a high vis shirt, then went to work.

Chapter 3: Zero bars

It's never easy for a person to acknowledge that they are average. I can't speak for women, but for a man, it can be crushing.

Men grow up planning to be rock stars, astronauts, high paid athletes…, superheroes. So, while there are some who are special and achieve those things, sadly, most of us do not.

I live in an average house, in a middle-class suburb. I have a normal job, and I'm an ok husband. I'm a pretty good dad who's raised some pretty good kids.

I'm just a regular guy. Could I change some things? Sure, who couldn't? I like who I am though, I'm a decent person, there's nothing wrong with me, I am just not extraordinary. There's nothing extra or particularly special about me. I recognize that to most people, I'm just a face in a crowd full of faces.

Now, I do say all these things with a caveat. My brain is, in fact, extraordinary, as I am a lot smarter than the majority of people, but that isn't something that's tangible from across the room. My brain doesn't walk through a door and make women look up from their phones. It doesn't make men sit up straighter or cause their voices to drop an octave when talking to me. In an intellectual setting, yes, but in regular everyday life, no.

That's what I was thinking about as I drove to the YMCA for the annual rules and regulations meeting for parents, coaches, and volunteers.

With all my kids grown and done with sports, I felt like I still had a little left in the tank as far as coaching and volunteering goes. If nothing else, I'm an extra set of hands.

I arrived a few minutes early, engaged in some friendly small talk with people I had volunteered with in the past, then took my seat and patiently waited for Director Douglas to come in and start the meeting.

That's when I heard it. That unmistakable baritone coming from the exact type of person I was just thinking about on the way here.

Willie Nash stepped through the door laughing and joking with the director about how much weight they bench pressed, or how many beers they drank, or how many different women they slept with in the last week.

Side note, I don't actually know what they were saying, but what else do bro's talk about?

Willie shook everyone's hand and genuinely seemed to care when he asked them how they were doing, as he stopped and gave each individual person their own time. He made it to my side of the room, and even though he apologized for forgetting my last name, he remembered my first, asked how my kids were doing, then even went so far as to congratulate me on my first grandchild.

He was the type of person who had 'it', and whatever 'it' was, he had it in spades. Whether it was his charming personality, his fork-tongued quick wit, or the muscles that he couldn't hide with double XL t-shirts, he was a lightning rod. Maybe it was his rugged good looks... he was just one of those people.

And I'm not even gay, not that there's anything wrong with that, but let's just be honest, this guy fell into the good side of the gene pool. Men wanted to be him, women wanted to be with him. It is what it is.

With all that being said, the truth was that Willie Nash was actually a good guy, and I genuinely liked him as a person. We'd worked together before and were signed up for a lot of the same programs. Our core values, when it came to coaching youth athletics, were in line with one another, so it was an easy pairing.

The meeting was the same as it was every year, the exception being that this year's background checks would also include taking fingerprints from all participants. There was a surprising amount of pushback aimed at Director Douglas and this new policy.

Of course, it was Willie Nash who stood up and said, "Ladies and gentlemen, if you are worried about your fingerprints being documented, then being tracked by the government, you shouldn't be carrying a cell phone. If you're worried about being exposed for some minor infractions from your past, they might have a problem with that," he looked at the director, "although I'm sure you can figure that out and work through it. But if you're worried about being exposed for something you've done to children, I personally have a problem with you, and we can deal with that right now." He looked into every eyeball in the room. As aggressive as that statement was, it didn't come off as a threat. He made his point, then smiled, "And for everyone else who has nothing to hide, who's down for some Buffalo wild wings after this?" Everyone cheered, and no one said another word about fingerprints. I had to admit, I was a Willie Nash fan.

I agreed to meet up with everyone for some wings and to have a few beers, but stayed behind to help clean up. A woman named Carol stayed behind as well to ask me some questions regarding her son. I'd known the family for years as a coach since her son Manny was in grade school. Carol, now divorced, said Manny was getting harder and harder to control. He was acting out in school, his grades were slipping, and to me, he was just going through the basic things boys go through during puberty. She was an attractive enough woman who played with her hair too much and kept touching my arm as she spoke.

She wanted some advice and wondered if I had extra time to maybe mentor and/or tutor her son. She went on and on about me being a good role model, and how he'd always responded well to my coaching style. The conversation changed somewhat when she spoke about how lucky my kids were to have a dad like me, and how appreciative my wife must be to have a husband like me. She reminded me several times that she was now single and had plenty of free time.

She continued to talk in the parking lot as I walked her to her car. We'd already agreed to meet up at the restaurant with everyone else, so why she felt the need to carry on like this, here, was beyond me.

"I have to get gas, then I'll be over there. See you in a minute, Carol!" I waved, then got into my vehicle, replaying the conversation in my head. "I really am a pretty good coach, though!" I laughed to the rearview mirror as I backed out.

I filled up the tank quickly, then headed to Buffalo Wild Wings, deciding to take the back roads, which were longer in distance, but would get me there quicker since there were no stoplights and rarely any other vehicles.

I tried to call my wife to let her know where I was going and ask if she'd like to join us, but couldn't get any signal. I looked at my phone, no bars. It was like a new school rapper, zero bars. I laughed to myself. My kids would've gotten a kick out of that joke. This road is like a bad college town, zero bars.

Ha ha, I could do this all day, I thought. This road will never have any alcoholics on it, there's no bars!

"Ok, dad, we get it…" I could see the eye rolls.

This road is like… I saw flashing lights ahead. Someone had pulled their car to the side of the street and had their hazards on. I slowed down to see if I could be of any assistance. My brain spoke first, as I rolled down my window, "Hey, look who it is!"

Chapter 4: Allergies

Willie Nash knelt down and looked at his rear passenger side tire. My brain quickly assessed his situation. Flat tire, wrong equipment, frustrated guy. I backed my car behind his and parked at a slight angle for safety.

"Whatcha got?" I asked, getting out and extending my hand.

"Fucking jack!" he said, squeezing my knuckles together, making sure I knew that his grip was stronger than mine.

I flinched at his choice of words but saw what he was talking about. The handle to his car jack laid broken in half on the ground.

"I mean, what's the fucking point of having a tool that can't do its job!" It wasn't a question that needed an answer. "FUCK!" He grabbed the jack and threw it across the street.

"Hey man, it's cool, I got one," I said, walking back to my truck.

"GRRR! I'm sorry, man, it's been a day." He walked across the road to pick up what he'd thrown and put it in his back seat.

I carried a floor jack from my vehicle and set it down next to his rear bumper, then knelt and started to put on a pair of latex gloves to keep my hands clean.

"Nope. No sir, I got it. Thanks, man, I got it. I can't have another man change my tire. It's not gonna happen! Ha ha!"

Of course, Mr. macho man.

"There's the release right there," I said, pointing to the side of the hydraulic jack.

"I got it," he replied smugly.

He knelt as I stood and began positioning the jack underneath the vehicle.

"I got an extra pair of gloves for you," I said, although at this point, I could have just put 'em back where they came from. Apparently, real men don't wear gloves.

"I'm allergic to latex. Ha ha ha!" He gave me a poop eating grin and a wink, then began the process of removing the tire.

The comment took me back mentally to a place I hadn't been in a long time. Willie Nash talked as he worked... something about protein powder versus real food, but I wasn't paying attention. I was lost in the memory of a 13-year-old kid, riding in a car with one of my mom's boyfriends.

"You got a girlfriend?"

"Yes."

"You knock her down yet?"

"Huh?"

"You-knock-her- down- yet? Have-y'all had- sex?" He spoke slower, like he was mentally challenged, twisting his hand with each syllable. I'd heard what he said, I just didn't understand the question.

"Oh, no!" I hadn't even held her hand yet. I was uncomfortable with this conversation.

"Do it, soon. Hit it and quit it. If she lets you do it, leave her, she's trash. Or she'll fall in love, and she'll want you to talk to her every day."

"But...."

"Charlie Tuna," I hated that nickname by the way, "trust me. Nothing is more annoying than listening to a woman talk. All they do is nag and complain. Picture this. You know how you're playing your game, and your mom tells you to come take out the trash, and you say you will, right after the game, but she wants it done right then?"

"Yeah…" I answered. She did that all the time. It was so annoying.

"Imagine that, every single time she speaks, for the rest of your life," he said, pointing his finger at every word for emphasis.

I opened the window to avoid coughing from his cigarette smoke. If I coughed, it would start a whole round of him teasing me, calling me a sissy, and saying I had baby lungs. He said only immigrants were scared of cancer.

"You got rubbers?"

"Yes, I have one my dad gave me."

He side eyed me before he spoke. "Bring it with you, but at the last minute, tell her that you're allergic to latex." He flashed me a poop eating grin and winked, proud of himself for being the one to share this treasure trove of knowledge. "She won't make you wear it if you say that."

We rode in silence the rest of the way to football practice.

"Hey," he said as I unloaded my gear from the backseat, "make sure you pull out."

"What?" I asked.

"When y'all having sex, and you about to bust, pull out. You don't want her to get pregnant, kids suck, they ruin everything. Just pull out and you'll be ok." He flicked his cigarette at me and drove away.

I stood there, completely confused, watching as he sped off in my mom's car.

By the time I had snapped back to reality, I was kneeling next to Willie Nash, who was stretched out, lying on his back, halfway underneath the car, cussing about a stripped-out lug bolt.

I was still wearing my latex gloves when I pressed the release valve on the jack. The car fell, landing on the heavily muscled upper torso of my volunteer friend. I heard bones break as he let out a squeal that sounded surprisingly feminine.

His legs kicked out once, and his hands grabbed for anything as he struggled to live. I was holding a four inch pocketknife that I must've grabbed from my toolkit while I was lost in my memorles.

I stabbed the man in his chest and abdomen repeatedly, unsure if the blade could even penetrate deep enough to reach any vital organs. I sliced a hole, then used my fingers to try and push through the chest cavity. I was trying to feel if his heart was still beating. I don't think it was.

My brain thought it would be funny to cut the middle fingers off the latex gloves I had offered and leave them stuck in the wound that used to be his belly button. I didn't. That would just be cruel and unnecessary.

"Talk about overkill," I said to myself.

I went back to my car and changed into a spare set of clothes that I kept in a gym bag on the floor behind my passenger

27

seat. Ironically, it was my referee outfit, zebra stripes and all. I put it on, then drove to Buffalo Wild Wings.

I went in through the side door, then to the restroom, hoping no one would see me before I had a chance to wash my hands and face. Satisfied that I was clean enough, I walked into the dining area where everyone from the meeting was already sitting and blew my referee whistle. I put on a silly show of calling fouls and doing the over-the-top hand signals that referees are known for doing.

Everyone laughed and joined in on the fun, launching good natured jokes at me, then one another, as we ate wings and drank beer. I felt good, I was having fun. For those few hours, I felt like 'the man.'

Driving home, I wondered if that was how Willie Nash felt every day.

Chapter 5: 48 hours

"Did you hear about Miss Kara?" Jermaine asked.

"Who?" I asked, even though I knew the answer.

"Miss Kara. You know, the older lady on line 6?"

"You mean Miss Carla?" I was annoyed. It was too early for gossip.

"Yeah, they saying she killed her husband and ran off," he said.

"Whaaat? No way. Oh yeah? No, I didn't know. That's crazy!" I'd already had this conversation 4 times, and I'd only been at work 20 minutes.

That's all everyone was talking about.

Moneca, the shift lead, called an emergency plant meeting to let us all know what was going on. She said the company was cooperating with police, and detectives would be here later to question each of us. She assured us that we were not suspects, they just needed to gather as much information as possible to catch the killer. She noted that we didn't have to speak to them, and, if we had legal representation, we could use them. Her personal opinion was to just get it over with. "If you ain't got nothing to do with it, you ain't got shit to worry about. Fighting it would just look like guilt, but do whatever y'all want!"

My brain accepted the challenge.

I got the notice shortly after noon when it was my turn to be questioned.

"Hey," I said, acting annoyed, even though I was anything but. I stepped into an office, sat in a chair across the table from an investigator who introduced himself as Detective Lucas. Our HR lady, Evelyn, sat in the corner, observing.

"Evil Lyn," I said under my breath. I nodded dismissively in her direction.

"What's that?" Detective Lucas asked.

"Nothing," I replied.

Detective Lucas was a tiny man. I wondered if his feet even touched the floor as he sat down. He had a folder with my name on it open in front of him.

"Do I know you from somewhere?" I asked.

"I don't know, do you? Have you ever been in trouble?" He replied condescendingly.

Okay, the game begins.

"Nope, never was. But you already know that." I looked at my file sitting on the table, then at him, matching his glare.

"But you do look familiar," I said again. I couldn't place it. It was on the tip of my tongue... YouTube? The Internet? Maybe a commercial on TV...? I'd seen him somewhere.

"So, what do you want to know?" I asked.

"What was your relationship with Carla?"

"I didn't have a relationship with Carla, she's a married woman."

We sat staring at each other.

"You're on TV, ain't you?" I broke the stalemate.

He continued his stare.

"Are you on TV?" I asked again.

"Yes," he finally answered.

"Oh! I know you're on that 48-hour show, right? First 48! You're that detective guy," I said excitedly, looking from him to the HR lady.

"You got me," he said, holding his hands up. "So, you're a fan, I take it?"

"Nope, not at all. My wife watches it. I think it's trash TV."

"What's so bad about it?" he countered, "I'm just doing my job." He played offended, to my insulting. We danced perfectly.

"You make money off of people's misery, it sucks," I answered, yawning disrespectfully.

"No, I'm literally just doing my job, and they follow me with cameras. I didn't kill anybody. I'm trying to find the killers and bring justice to the families."

"Oh, you don't get extra money from the show, my apologies, I just assumed..."

"Well, I do, obviously. I mean, it's TV," he said.

"So, you get paid off of people's misery." It was a statement, not a question.

"Listen, I'm the good guy here."

I ignored his comment and continued my point. "So I should have a TV show too, then. I'm just doing my job... Why isn't anyone following me, recording me on the production line?"

I looked at Evelyn, who was sitting forward, intrigued by the verbal pugilism.

"Charles, look, I'm just trying to find a killer."

Another pregnant pause.

"So, what do you actually want to know, Mr. TV star?" I relented.

"What was your relationship with Carla?"

"She was a co-worker, that's it."

"It shows that you were late on the day of the murder..." He let his words hang, wanting me to grab them.

I didn't.

"And...?" he did a hand gesture that I took to mean, 'go on...'

"And what? Oh, was that a question? Yes, I had car troubles," I said with a smirk.

"Did you see anything?" He asked.

"Regarding...?" I did his own 'go on' hand gesture back to him. "Are you asking if I saw a murder? No, I didn't see a murder. But what I did see was a woman who came to work with a different bruise every other week. We all knew Miss Carla was in an abusive relationship." I looked at the HR lady again, "So if she killed her husband, he probably deserved it. My mom was abused..."

I stopped. I had said too much.

"Are we done here? I have work to do!" I stood. Detective Lucas also stood. I walked to the door.

"One more question, Charles, please."

I exhaled loudly to show my irritation, but stopped in the doorway.

"Where do you fish at?"

"Huh?" Where did that come from, I wondered.

"I read your bio," he pushed my folder towards the middle of the table, "under interests, it says hobbies, fishing, and mountain biking. I've been known to take a few croppy out the water... I'm just wondering if you had a honey hole or somewhere I haven't been. Maybe you could show me a few spots."

His question caught me off guard, and he knew it. His whole demeanor changed. It was like he regained control of the conversation.

"It's Lucas, right?" I asked, regaining my footing. Using the old, 'act like I don't remember his name' trick, I was trying to ruffle his feathers, respectfully.

"DETECTIVE, Lucas." He wanted his respect.

"A real fisherman would never ask about another's honey hole. Good try though."

I walked out into the hallway, waited a minute, then poked my head back in the door, "Hey, how was that? Am I gonna be on TV? That's what you needed for the show, right? Drama?"

The detective looked confused.

"Can we take a selfie? My wife will be so impressed. I might even get some tonight!" I pulled out my phone, held it up, turned, and took the selfie with an unamused Detective Lucas in the background.

The rest of my shift felt like it should be in the Guinness book of World Records for the longest shift ever. When it was finally done, I drove my exhausted body to the gas station at the end of the road for a 5-hour energy and a cup of the world's worst coffee. As I poured my cup, I saw Evil Lyn walk through the front door. I turned and walked to the back of the store, then crouched down, pretending to look at items on the bottom shelf, hoping not to be recognized.

I heard her ask for a carton of Marlboro reds, heard the cashier say, 'thank you, come again', then heard the bell of the front door. Feeling like I'd made it unnoticed, I stood and accidentally bumped into the person behind me.

"Oh! Sorry! My bad, I didn't…"

I never had the chance to finish my apology when Miss Evelyn, Miss HR (which stood for horror to the people on the factory floor), was standing so close to me, I could feel the heat from her nicotined body, encroaching on my personal space.

"BLEGH!" I fake vomited, then took a step to the side to allow myself a breath of fresh air.

"That was cute today, Mr. Brown. So, to be clear, you WANT to be a suspect?"

"What?" I was confused by her question.

"You could've just played it straight. You could've just said, yes, no, no, yes, whatever, and just been done with it and moved on. But you had to make it a show. He HAS to investigate you now, which means I have to do more fucking work digging through your history, while these assholes stand over my shoulder watching me, making sure I'm doing my job correctly!"

I flinched at her choice of words.

She continued, "We watch the same shows, you know. We saw what you were trying to do. How to get away with murder, season 2, episode 3. Sooo obvious! Do you want us to think you're a killer? Why? For what? Have you ever killed anything, Charles? Have you! You're the type who vacuums spiders so you don't hurt them. You've added so much work to my desk!" She staggered those last few words as if pleading for me to take it all back. "Did you watch Dexter, Charles? Do you watch....? Oh my God! What am I saying, of course you watched Dexter! Ugh!" She was having a breakdown. "You are so... why do you fucking people act like this? Just do your jobs. Just do your fucking jobs!" She stormed away, out of breath

I laughed to myself, because even though she didn't have a lit cigarette, a cloud of smoke followed her the same way as the cloud of dust followed Pig Pen in the comic strip.

My brain told me to follow her.

I had a new burst of energy. I put down my items, then hurried outside just in time to see Evil Lyn put on her helmet and climb on top of her motor scooter.

Chapter 6: Vespa

I'm not a hunter anymore. I don't stalk my prey. I'm not like any of those guys in those documentaries that has this uncontrollable lust for death. There are no reasons for me to continue doing what I do. There are no 'triggers' per se. I can go years in between taking someone. I simply wait until an opportunity presents itself. I've matured.

Evil Lyn was different. This was personal. She was not a nice person, often bullying people, using her status to push people around. I didn't like her before, but then this little incident at the store and her insinuating that I was a suspect in Carla's death made me want to take her. She pretty much sealed her fate. She should've just gotten her cancer sticks, caught said disease, and died of 'natural' causes. She should've just went on her way. I had to take her. It reminded me of when I was younger, and the only way to calm down was to kill something.

I remember when I was like every other normal teenage boy who fantasized about killing prostitutes, like my mom's old friends. They were all whores and even at that young age, I realized how lonely and desperate they were. I knew I would be doing them a favor. Back then, I had planned on setting them all free from their pain and suffering.

I used to wait in the shadows until they were done with whatever guy they were with, then attack. None of the women ever suspected it was me since a lot of them helped raise me as a child. I called most of them auntie. Auntie Lisa, Auntie Mary, etcetera, etcetera. They trusted me, so it was easy to get close and just slice 'em up with an old barbers' knife I stole from one of my mom's regulars.

I learned quickly. I started off doing easy, 'humane' killings, then really started to enjoy it, so I began experimenting. For instance, cutting left to right across the neck was known as the silent scream; no sound would come out. Cutting vertically instead of horizontally down the femoral artery, the main artery that runs down the leg, was a slower bleed out, but more painful. You had to be precise.

I was freeing the women, I was doing them a service, but I was murdering the men. I absolutely hated men back then. Men are the worst. The way they treated women. The way they walked around doing whatever they wanted, to whoever they wanted to do it to. I hated the way they treated my mom, it was just cruel and unnecessary. I enjoyed giving them what they gave those ladies.

It was with the men that I learned to hunt. I learned how to watch people. I figured out how to read body language and mannerisms. I found out that humans are creatures of habit. If people are given a choice in a situation, and all things are equal, most people will continue to do the same thing they've always done. Even at my job, people tend to park in the same spots, week after week, year after year, for no other reason than they did it the day before.

Another thing I learned, and always thought was funny, was how these so-called macho men cried a whole lot more than any woman when it came to pain. I would often have to take them quickly just because of all the yelling and hollering they did.

It was hard following Evil Lin because she rode that stupid scooter so slowly. I tried to remain incognito, but cars would honk, then go around her, leaving me exposed as the lone vehicle on the road. My original plan was to follow her home, then, based on the info I collected, figure out the best way to take her. But I knew this stretch of two lane roadway like the back of my hand.

My brain set it up perfectly. I slowed my car down to 15 miles per hour below the speed limit until there were 4 cars behind me. I would accelerate when they tried to pass. My goal was to upset them to the point that they would speed past me and still be irritated enough to speed past her. It worked perfectly. The irritated drivers accelerated past both of us as a group. I was the only one left, and with no other cars in sight, I sped up on the side of her and pulled my wheel hard to the right, cutting her off, causing her to go off the road, down an embankment, and crash into a tree.

By the time I parked and made it down to where she was, it looked like she'd already taken her last breath. I removed her helmet and bashed her face with it anyway. Overkill? Yes. Unnecessary and cruel? Also yes.

I climbed the hill back to my truck and sat for a minute, trying to control my breathing. Even though I've done it hundreds of times, taking a life was always exhilarating; it took a lot out of me. I was back to being exhausted. I made a U-turn, going back to the store where I left my 5-Hour Energy.

Chapter 7: Director's Cut part 1

Traffic was terrible as expected, and I made it home with just enough time to shower, eat, and then dress for a night of refereeing high school basketball.

I pulled into the YMCA's parking lot and saw several police cars with their lights flashing, parked by the front door. I walked up to the entrance, stopping to talk to shocked looking employees who were standing off to the side, speaking in whispered tones.

"Willie Nash was murdered!" Justin said.

"I just saw him yesterday!" Edgar said.

"Oh my God, I can't believe it," said Chelsea.

"IT WASN'T ME! I WAS AT THE RESTAURANT! ASK THEM! JUST ASK THEM!" YMCA Director Douglas was being dragged through the door by police, accused of murdering Willie Nash. He saw me.

"CHARLES! ASK CHARLES! HEY, TELL THEM! I WAS AT THE RESTAURANT! WE WERE AT THE RESTAURANT!"

I pretended like I didn't know what was happening and kept my mouth closed as he was led away. They were pushing him into the back of a squad car when he began to fight. He went from pleading to demanding, he be let free, screaming his innocence, refusing to be arrested. In his struggle, he accidently head butted the female officer, then landed a solid kick to the groin of her partner as he took off running.

"FREEZE! PUT YOUR HANDS UP!" A third officer ran out of the building, gun raised, yelling his demand.

The director stopped and turned to face him. "Please don't shoot me, Mr. Officer. Please, don't shoot me, man. Please. Can you not shoot me, man?"

"PUT YOUR FUCKING HANDS UP! NOW!" the cop yelled.

"I'm not going to do nothing ... I'm sorry, Mr. Officer, I'll get on my knees, whatever," the director begged.

"HANDS!" the officer yelled again.

"I CAN'T!" he yelled, twisting his body to show that he couldn't because of the handcuffs.

Someone yelled, "GUN!"

POP! POP! POP! The officer, yelling commands, shot him.

POP! POP! POP! The officer who was kicked, shot, too.

There was a short pause, then, **POP! POP!** The female officer added her unnecessary two cents.

"NO! NO! STOP! CEASE FIRE! CEASE FIRE!"

Detective Lucas came running from the building, towards the handcuffed man, who lay motionless, face down on the pavement. Everything else stopped. It was like someone pressed pause on a movie.

I immediately replayed the scene in my head, now seeing it in slow motion. When Director Douglas twisted to show that he couldn't put his hands up, the cuffs reflected the light from the YMCA sign at such an angle that from a certain perspective, it kind of looked like a chrome-plated pistol.

He'd been hit squarely by 8 shots at close range, so by the time Detective Lucas reached him, he didn't even try doing CPR; there was no need. He knelt over the body with his head down, lips moving as if saying a prayer.

He raised his head, then whoever had pressed pause in this movie had now pressed play, and turned the volume up to 20.

Everyone ran in different directions. Women screamed, kids cried, men hollered, sirens blared, and lights flashed on and off. All at the same time!

Detective Lucas did his best to control the scene, and it only took a look from him to push me into action, barking orders for people to back up, move the kids inside.

"You, take this there! You, put that here! Now! GO!"

We covered the body. We set up barriers. We yellow-taped the parking lot. I helped investigators with a list of witnesses. We pushed back the press. I took a group of young employees and had a heart to heart in a separate room, explaining what happened and what they should do now as far as counseling and talking through their feelings. It was hectic until support came, but together, we got it done.

"Thanks, man," Detective Lucas extended his hand and grasped mine with a grip far firmer than his size would imply.

"You're welcome," I said, before adding, "he was a good man, he didn't deserve that."

"He wasn't even a suspect," the detective said, wiping his eyes, exhausted.

I looked over at him.

"He had traffic tickets."

"Ha, figures," I said, remembering his affinity for speeding. "That's his Tesla outside. Those things are faster than they look. Believe me."

"Anyways," he continued, "Officer Griner remembered him from a traffic stop, and whatever happened there carried over to here. We were just asking about Willie... She was the aggressor. She must have been juiced up on her testosterone or something because she put him in cuffs, then, for whatever reason, he started yelling about not being a murderer. I don't know... it escalated... quickly! I should've stopped it, I should've done more. I don't think I'll be able to sleep for a while with this on my conscience."

We stood in silence, both of us deep in thought.

He looked at his watch. "It's too late for a drink. You busy tomorrow? I'll get the first 5 or 6 rounds... I appreciate the help, you're a natural. I have some ideas I'd like to throw at you."

I looked around at the now-organized chaos still going on. My eyes concentrated on the spot where Director Douglas still lay. "Yeah," I said solemnly, "Sure, why not?"

I drove home in silence. My brain wasn't the emotional type, but I couldn't help but feel at least partially responsible for the director's death. He really was a good guy, I lost a friend that night.

I knew my wife would still be awake when I walked in. She'd texted me earlier about a new story by her favorite author that she was excited to read. Emerson's Island or something to that effect.

"Hey," I said quietly, crawling into bed next to her. I looked over and saw my clothes for tomorrow's work day, folded neatly on the dresser.

She took a sip from the glass of wine, then said, "I saw you on the news, you ok?" She patted me on the thigh but didn't say anything else. She knew I didn't want to talk, but that when I was ready, I'd fill her in on every detail. She was a good woman, and I loved her with all my heart. Almost all of my friends at one point or another have said that I've outkicked my coverage when it came to her. A football analogy that basically meant she was too good for me.

I've always said that one of the best parts about being married to someone for a long time is the fact that you know each other's likes and dislikes. You know their wants and needs without asking. In this case, she knew that what I wanted was just any part of her body touching mine. It was the comfort I needed, and I fell asleep as soon as my head hit the pillow.

Chapter 7: Director's Cut part 2

BANG! BANG! BANG!

I woke up to the sound of someone pounding on the front door. I instinctively grabbed the pistol off my nightstand, angry about being woken up.

BANG! BANG! BANG!

"POLICE! OPEN UP!"

"Get dressed, get under the bed!" I told my wife, just in case they wanted to shoot first. RIP Atatiana.

"HOLD ON!" I yelled, "I'M COMING!"

I pulled on a pair of sweatpants, passed the pistol to my wife, and moved quickly towards the front door.

"BOOM!"

The door exploded into a million pieces as people in riot gear burst through the entrance, pointing large automatic weapons in every different direction.

I was already headed back to the bedroom when I heard Detective Lucas's voice yelling, "CHARLES! CHARLES BROWN! WE HAVE THE HOUSE SURROUNDED! PUT YOUR HANDS UP, SURRENDER!"

"WHAT DO YOU WANT FROM ME, DETECTIVE? I DIDN'T DO ANYTHING!" I yelled back.

"We know it was you, Charles. We know what you did! Come on out. Nobody needs to get hurt!"

"What is he talking about?" my wife asked from under the bed. I didn't respond.

"I didn't do anything, detective," I said again, trying to remain calm.

"Charles, listen. We are taking you in. I have orders, dead or alive. Open the door."

I turned, grabbed my shotgun from the closet, and then racked it. I knew that even to an untrained ear, the CLACK CLACK sound of a pump shotgun is as unmistakable as the sound of a diamondback rattlesnake's rattle in the Arizona desert.

"OPEN THE DOOR, CHARLES! OPEN THE DOOR! OPEN THE FUCKING..."

BOOM!

I shot. Double-aught buckshot shattered the door instantly.

Silence....

I got low, crawling under the bed with my wife. I knew what was coming.

The cops opened fire in the bedroom, letting off an impressive number of rounds, though none hit their intended target, me.

"CEASE FIRE! CEASE FIRE!" Detective Lucas begged. "STOOOOPPPP!"

Silence...

"OK! ENOUGH. I'M COMING!" I yelled, setting the shotgun down.

I waved a rag in front of the door just to test that they weren't going to shoot anything that moved.

"I'm coming out! Don't shoot!" I said again.

I grabbed a handful of my wife's hair and pulled her up. I moved into the doorway, dragging her aggressively by the neck, pistol to her head.

"Charles! What the hell are you doing?" Detective Lucas asked.

"I'm leaving! Tell your guys to get back!"

"CHARLES! LET HER GO!" The look of confusion on the detective's face was priceless.

"OW! That hurts! What are you doing? Stop!" My wife pleaded. She looked at the cops, "HELP ME!" Her cries were real.

I hit her on the head with the butt of my pistol, "SHUT UP!" I demanded.

Every gun was aimed at me as I dragged her to the front door.

"Put the weapons down," I said, still moving.

My wife continued to beg. "Shoot him! Help me!" I hit her again, but this time it was for burning my toast at breakfast the previous morning. Another benefit of a long marriage is knowing how dark a piece of bread should be toasted. I feel like she burned it on purpose.

"Charles, you're not going to get away with this," Detective Lucas said, as I grabbed my key and then forced her into the truck.

"I hear murder suicide is nice this time of year. How many deaths can you be directly involved with in one night, detective? How's your conscience gonna sleep now?" I said before getting in on the driver's side.

I sped away knowing I'd be followed.

Sadly, my brain abandoned me, I was on my own, and I didn't have a plan. There was no endgame at this point. The only things I knew right now was that they knew about the murders, and the lady to my right was crying too much. Hitting her was only making it worse.

"Baby, please, I can't think with all that noise." She didn't stop.

"Babe... please..." I tried again.

"Why are you doing this?" she cried. "Why are you treating me like this? Why did you hit me?"

I looked at her when she said that, but continued to drive aimlessly, knowing that the number of police behind me had grown exponentially.

"I've done some bad things..."

My wife finally quieted down, "Like what? What does that mean?"

"Those murders... the ones all over the news.... That was me," I confessed.

"What? Ha ha. Shut up! You couldn't kill anything. You?" She dismissed me with a disrespectful wave of the hand.

"You're a weak, spineless fool. A killer? Ha!"

The more she said, the faster I drove.

"You're a coward. You've always been a coward. Your dad was right, he wanted a son but got you!"

That stung, but didn't stop me.

"You're a loser.... And now you're a woman-beating loser."

Still didn't stop me.

"A killer...? That's good. What else are you? Oh, I know, a clown! You're a fucking..."

That did it!

I cut my wheel hard to the right. My truck crashed through the guardrail and went over the edge of the bridge we were riding on, then fell 200 feet down towards the river below us.

As we dropped, time stopped. There was peace in the weightlessness. It was a euphoric, almost orgasmic experience. The truck tumbled beautifully as the best parts of my life flashed before my eyes.

The same could not be said for my wife, who screamed a silent scream of horror, as both her paralyzing fear of heights and water were being realized at the same time.

SPLASH!

The water was warm. It had a stickiness to it that was unexpected. I felt it trickle down the back of my head, to my neck...

"OH MY GOD! BABE, I'M SO SORRY!"

I sat up, confused.

"Babe, I didn't mean to. I fell asleep with the glass in my hand. I didn't mean to wake you! Oh my God, I'm such a klutz! Let me...don't move, let me grab a towel..."

"What?" Sleep still had hold of me.

"I'm so sorry," my wife said again, as she wiped me off and did her best to dry the bed.

By the time I'd realized what happened and what she was saying, I had already laid my head back down and was onto my next dream.

Chapter 8: Inside Man

I told my wife about my dream the next morning, over a hot cup of coffee, eggs sunny side up, and 2 pieces of bread, toasted perfectly to a nice golden brown.

She laughed at the part about me grabbing her by the hair and dragging her through the front door. She laughed even harder and choked on her food at the part about me bopping her on the head with my pistol. Her exact words: "I wish you would try to hit me on the head! Just go on and shoot me dead, cuz ah, looka here, we both going to jail if that happens." She snapped her fingers as she talked.

I believed her.

I said that I was going to be late coming home since I'd be at the bar with Detective Lucas, and she replied by telling me not to forget about the early start we had the next day.

"Oh snap! I forgot all about that! Vacation! Vacation!" I stood, grabbed her politely by the hand, and began to dance around the kitchen, singing the Beach Boys song, "Montego, Aledo, baby, why don't we go... Bermuda, Bahama, come on pretty mama... Eat Fritos in my Speedo, baby, why don't we go..." I didn't know the words, but she giggled and danced with me anyway, before I caught a glimpse of the time and had to hurry up and go.

"Go get my seat warm," I demanded, tossing my keys at her. She let them hit the floor without any attempt to make the catch. "Pick 'em up, NOW!" I walked over and reached to grab her by the hair.

"Boy, if you don't get your silly butt away from me!" She ducked under my hand and gave me a quick kiss on the cheek, laughing and smacking my rear end as she did. "Don't let your dream self get your real self beat up!"

"Ha ha, ok. Love you, see you tonight," I said, walking away. "Bermuda, Bahama, I'm sleeping with your mama..."

My day at work went by fast since I didn't let anything bother me. I was focused on my vacation.

After work at the bar, the detective and I argued about every topic, from religion in school to the greatest basketball player of all time. Our longest discussion centered around whether Cowboys owner Jerry Jones was the reason for the team's failures.

I was enjoying myself. I liked the detective, we became fast friends. We both did our best to keep things light, although the elephant in the room remained. He told me that he needed someone to bounce ideas off of. A civilian, with no ties that bind. He felt that he'd been doing his job for so long, he couldn't see reality anymore. He saw everything through 'thin blue line' tinted glasses. He needed an outside ear.

"Can I trust you?"

"Yes."

A bond was formed. We sealed it with a clink of our beer mugs and by downing the rest of our drinks.

"I don't like that bitch!" he said. Out of nowhere.

I flinched.

"Who?" I looked around to see who he was talking about.

"That Griner bitch. Yesterday was her fault. She was the one who killed your friend. I think it's the meds. She takes those testosterone pills, and it gives her roid rage. She's way too aggressive with people. But hey, we're a team, right? Gotta back the blue, right?"

"Do you? I mean, look, you're grown, but..." I paused searching for the right words. "There's a Malcolm X quote that's always stuck with me. The older I get, the truer it is. He said, 'I have more respect for a man who lets me know where he stands, even if he's wrong, than the one who comes up like an angel and is nothing but a devil.' You. Detective Lucas, need to pick a side."

He sat, quiet, deep in thought, feeling the alcohol.

I stood and tossed money on the bar, "That's for the tip. I gotta go." We shook hands, and I walked away.

"Hey!" he called after me. I walked back to him.

"Hey, I forgot to tell you, we found your lady."

I just stared at him.

"Your lady. Your HR lady," he was slurring his words. "She crashed into a tree on her scooter."

"I heard. That sucks. Talk to you later." I was ready to leave. My brain wanted to stay and play.

"Wait, please. What have you heard? I got nothing. No leads and nobody seems to know anything about anything. Please..."

"I don't know, just stuff. Like, her face was mashed up pretty bad, died immediately, or whatever. I don't know, I don't pay attention to gossip. I really don't care."

He stared at me, searching...

I looked up at the bartender, "Hey, don't let him drive, ok?"

I met Detective Lucas at his office early the next morning. I promised my wife I'd be back in 2 hours, so I had to skip the small talk and get down to business. He said he understood and passed me a cup of coffee.

"So my first question to you is, do you know anyone that Carla was involved with? Did she have a boyfriend? A girlfriend? I mean, I know people have 'work husbands' or whatever, but I'm just trying to make sense of it all."

"No, not that I know of. But, I wouldn't know. I'm not the gossip type, like I said before. I have a very low tolerance for nonsense, so I don't deal with it."

"I get that, but follow me for a second. A woman gets in an argument with her abusive husband on the way to work. She

54

demands he stop the car. Maybe she knows there's a pistol in the glove box, whatever, so when he hits her, she shoots him, gets out, and just disappears into thin air?" he stopped talking.

I looked at him, not sure what he wanted from me. But I threw this out, "That doesn't make sense unless, like you said, she had a lover, or someone to pick her up. Did she have siblings? Maybe a family member was tired of hearing her cry to them about him?" I said, trying to sound neutral.

"I thought that too. But then why hide, right? The threat is gone. There's nothing to hide from at that point," he said, tapping his finger deep in thought.

"Right," I agreed. "Plus, why do it in the open? She could've lured him anywhere, killed him, and just acted like she never knew anything."

"Exactly. What if the husband's killer killed her too?"

"Why? That doesn't make sense. She was a nice lady. I didn't know her personal life, but I can't imagine her doing anything bad enough for someone to kill her. Wait, let me text someone who knows her," I said, reaching for my phone. I sent a text to a coworker, Leslie, who used to work side by side with Miss Carla. I asked if she had any information about their personal relationship.

She texted back that the husband had a pregnant girlfriend named Regan.

"That's your killer," I told the detective.

"Regan, huh? Ok, so we'll look for her. Thanks, man, I appreciate you coming in. It's a start." He stood and walked me out.

"What's next?" I asked as we passed through the front door.

"Well, I'm still waiting on the surveillance footage from the church where they found the car. They had security cameras everywhere, all over that place. Our tech guys are trying to clean up the video now."

I didn't react.

Chapter 9: Hot Cheetos

It's always a different experience riding in the passenger seat as opposed to driving. When you're driving, you're focused on the road. You're looking straight ahead, often missing the subtle details of your surroundings... The bike trail that ran along the highway, or cameras mounted on the streetlights under the overpass. I finally learned to trust my wife's extra slow, nervous, clogging up traffic driving style, so my brain was able to just relax and enjoy the ride.

Not one who particularly likes road trips, the drive to our ocean getaway was actually fun. We were both in good spirits and were being silly most of the way there. We sang along to old Prince songs, played the 'count the car color' road game, where the participant gets a point for each car with the color they chose that passed. We even played hi-lo with a deck of cards that were a permanent fixture in the vehicle. We laughed, we joked, we teased each other about our ages, and how many wrinkles we had.

"Oh, b.t.w, (I said the letters, not the words) were you planning on getting gas today or..?" I asked sarcastically, noticing that the gas light was on. She pulled up to a gas station in some random one-stoplight town off the freeway. I got out to pump while she rechecked the route and sang along to Little Red Corvette. I watched her through the window, she was still the cutest thing I'd ever laid eyes on.

"Truth or dare?" she asked, catching me looking at her.

"Dare. Of course."

"Go steal something," she said, laughing.

I didn't respond. I gave her my most playful, serious look, finished filling the tank, and then walked into the store.

It was a typical freeway gas station with snacks, postcards, snow globes with the name of the town, pocketknives, cell phone chargers... everything a traveler might need.

There were people already inside, which I was glad to see because it afforded me a distraction to make my move. I went quickly and decisively to the souvenir section, then grabbed a keychain knife with 'Charles' written on the side. It was exactly like the one I had years ago but lost. This one was a perfect replacement.

"Mom, can I get hot Cheetos?" a whiny teenager begged in the next aisle.

"Gerald dear, they upset your tummy, please find something else," a tired looking mother smiled apologetically in my direction. I smiled sympathetically back.

"MOM! I'M GETTING THESE GODDAMN CHEETOS!"

Whoa!

"Please, Gerald, we don't want you smelling up the car. Can it just wait?"

"BUY THE CHEETOS OLD LADY! DAD ALWAYS FARTS AND STINKS UP THE CAR. FAT BASTARD, I CAN TOO! BUY THE DAMN CHEETOS MOM!" He walked away. She didn't look embarrassed. She simply reached over, paid for the Cheetos, and rolled the stroller she was pushing to the front door, struggling with her arms full of items for their family.

I never understood how some parents allowed that type of disrespect. I'm not sure who needs the butt whooping more, the kids doing it, or the adults for letting them do it. It was never tolerated in my household. My brain processed the scene in slow motion as it happened in real time.

I shoved my new keychains in my pocket, then started towards the mom to lend a hand, but Gerald brushed past me, grabbed his bag from her, and walked away.

"Gerald, where are you going? We need to go now, your father's waiting."

He walked away, "I don't give a fuck, I have to take a shit!"

I flinched at his choice of words.

I grabbed 2 more keychain knives, one that said William and one that said Bill, and a snow globe, then followed the disrespectful teenager to the restroom.

"MMM Cheetos! I love that flavor," I said, as we walked in. I noticed both stall doors were open in the two-toilet bathroom, so I locked the door behind us.

"Hey!" he said, as I pushed him through the opening of the closest stall. He fell forward, hitting his head on the toilet seat cover dispenser, "OW! What the fuck man?"

I smashed the snow globe against the back of his head, causing him to fall and crumble onto the toilet. Hot Cheetos flew everywhere.

"How old are you, Gerald?" I asked calmly.

"What? Ow! Fuck you!"

I grabbed his hair and banged it against the toilet seat 3 times. Blood shot out of his face.

"Answer me," I said evenly.

"16! I'm 16, fuck!" He started to cry.

"Watch your mouth, boy!" I banged his head 3 more times, then dunked it in the toilet. The water turned red. My brain imagined that this was the same horror that 13-year-old girls saw the first time their 'friend' came for its monthly visit.

Gerald stayed motionless in that position, looking like he was bobbing for apples.

I turned around and grabbed a trash bag from the trash can, emptying its contents on the floor, then went back to the stall.

I pulled Gerald's bruised and bloodied 16-year-old head out of the water and wrapped the bag around it, twisting and squeezing it shut around his neck.

He instinctively reached and tried to pull it off, but I was much stronger than him. His deep breaths and screaming actually did more harm, since he was inhaling the plastic in deeper, sealing off his available airways.

I held him in that position for a minute or two after he stopped moving, then just let go, allowing his limp body to collapse back onto the toilet.

Leaving both the William and the Bill keychain knives stabbed into either side of his neck was admittedly overkill, but it wasn't as bad as the other option. My brain thought it would be funny to remove his shoestrings and tie his face to the bowl, then run out, grab a marker, and write 'potty mouth' on the kid's face. I thought that was unnecessary and cruel, so instead, I just sat him up and closed the door, that way if anyone walked in, it would look like a normal person doing their business.

I washed the blood off my hands and made sure to wipe down any surfaces that I touched with a towel. Not that it mattered, it was a public restroom.

I looked around the store nonchalantly to see if there were any cameras, knowing that a place like this might have one, but it would be aimed at the register, not the restroom. I grabbed a pair of oversized, extra dark, plastic sunglasses off the rack, and still wearing them, brought them to the counter and paid with cash.

"Oh, let me grab some peanuts and peppermints for the wife," I said, "she'll be pissed if I don't." The cashier smiled a knowing smile. I noticed his wedding ring.

I walked outside and saw Gerald's family sitting in a Dodge Caravan waiting impatiently for him to finish so they could be on their way.

"You're too soft on him. That's why he acts like that." I heard the dad argue.

"No, he's just sensitive. You're too hard on him," Mom replied.

I walked past and got into the passenger side of my truck.

"Bout time! I thought you got caught!" My better half complained.

"GO! GO!" I over exaggerated to make it seem like I robbed the store, and she was the getaway driver. She giggled as she pulled off, back onto the highway.

"What'd you get?" she asked excitedly.

I showed her my haul: 1 keychain, a bag of peppermints, peanuts...

"Awww heck! You did it! Let's hit a bank next! Ha ha! Wait, did you chicken out and pay for these? "

"No," I looked at her, "I mean, not really."

"Show me the receipt!" she joked. I didn't, we just laughed and continued our route.

"Hey, I had a taste for these, you want some?" I grabbed a handful of hot Cheetos, then passed her the bag.

Chapter 10: 16 Memory Ln

Dan and Dave were standing in their front yard, having a heated discussion, when we finally pulled into the driveway of our Oceanside beach house. Dave was waving his hands wildly, trying to explain something to his partner Dan, who stood with his hands on his hips, looking down at the grass.

They looked up and waved when they saw us. Dan made a beeline for our car. I heard him say, "Let's ask them."

"Hey y'all," he said, standing on the driver's side, waiting for my wife to get out.

They embraced before he came around to my side and gave me a hug, welcoming us.

"Ok, can you settle this for us? What looks better?" He looked down at his shoes. "Which one?"

"Ummm," I had no idea what he was talking about or what he wanted me to say.

Dave walked over, and after hugging my wife, said, "Will y'all tell this fool, please?"

"The right one!" My wife knew immediately. They all turned to me, waiting for my answer.

"Yeah, I'm uh, with her. The right one?"

"Boy, shut up!" Dan said, laughing and smacking me on the arm. They all laughed, I was clueless.

"Let me grab some bags... Dave? The bags?" Dan turned to look at his significant other, who was still joking with mine.

"No, I got 'em. Thank you, though. We only have a few," I said, opening the trunk.

"OK, muscles, we'll just watch then. Ha Ha!"

"Eyes up here, gentlemen! Eyes up here," My wife said, pushing her breasts out at them. They weren't interested, and we all started laughing again. "Where's Justin?"

"He went to pick up his trashy girlfriend, ugh. They'll be back any minute. Guuurrrll, don't get me started on that one," Dave said with a disgusted look.

63

"Please, don't!" Dan said, grabbing Dave by the arm and pulling him back over to their yard. "WE GOT MARAGRITAS BY THE GALLON Y'ALL. COME GET SOME!"

My wife told them she'd be over after a shower and a change of clothes. I brought the rest of our stuff in, threw it on the bed, then went to the kitchen for a beer. I was standing by the back window, looking at the water, when she came in with her wet hair pulled back in a ponytail. She gave me a kiss on the cheek, "I'm going over to Dan and Dave's, you going to be ok?"

"Yes," I let my answer hang, "gimme an hour. Don't drink it all!" She smiled. "Hey, what did I vote on outside?" I asked, still confused.

"Ha Ha, the way he tied his shoes. One shoe's laces were under the eyelets, the other's were over. We voted for the over."

I stood staring at her, more confused than before. She saw the look on my face, laughed, then, with another kiss and a "Hurry up," she was gone.

Dan and Dave had been our neighbors here since our kids were young. Over 15 years now. Dan has a son from his previous marriage who lives with them during the tourist months.

The son, Justin, had a different girlfriend every time we saw him, and part of our fun was meeting, then judging that poor girl.

I looked around and took in the familiarity. This was the home left to me by my father. His father left it to him, and so on. There were a lot of emotions that came with this place. I always took an hour or so to myself when we first got here, just so I could sort through my feelings and battle the demons that still lived within these walls. Once confronted and dealt with, I would be able to move on and enjoy my vacation.

I grabbed a new beer and went to sit on the deck. I got two texts back to back. One from my wife that said, 'She is not cute! At all!' I laughed, knowing she was talking about the new girlfriend.

The second text was from Detective Lucas, 'I got some news. Hit me back when you can.'

I turned the ringer off so I could concentrate on the sound of the water. It was hypnotizing.

My dad taught me how to listen to the ocean. He would tell me how most people just hear it with their ears, but if you can master your breathing and control your thoughts, you can feel the ocean. He said that a man's body is 60% water, so there's a natural rhythm that connects us to the sea. I remember taking walks with him and my mom. Up and down miles of shoreline in silence. The wind, the water, the sand... This was his happy place. A fisherman by trade, poetically, it would sound better to say he lost his life on the water, but that wasn't the case. He died in a car crash on the way to the boat. My mom was supposed to drop him off at the dock for his 2-week shift, but she was too drunk to drive. They argued, and she claims he hit her. He had to drive her home, which meant he was going to be late. I remember watching my mom stumble up the driveway, and him squealing the tires as he sped off...

I lost both parents that night. I have to remind myself that my mom wasn't bad. She was no Donna Morgan, I mean, there can only be one world's greatest mom, but she wasn't a bad mother. In hindsight, I was a bad kid. She was an alcoholic; that's her excuse. She loved her drink, she loved her sleep, and she said she loved me.

I blamed her for killing my dad. As a young kid, I was lost. I started acting out to get attention. When that stopped working, I became angry and violent. I remember she told me once that she was deathly afraid of spiders, so I went into the woods and collected as many as I could find for about a week. I waited till she was drunk and passed out in her room, and released all the spiders in her bed. I put some in her hair, under her shirt... It left me unsatisfied because she didn't even notice. Yeah, she had bites, but by the time she was actually coherent enough to know what was going on, the insects had all moved on.

I did all kinds of mean things to her: Tabasco in her toothpaste, needles in her shoes, I super-glued her two fingers together. And nothing... She never said anything about any of it. She just figured that she did it while she was drunk and couldn't remember.

Then came the boyfriends. By the time I was 13, there were so many guys that came and went, I stopped remembering names. Most of them ignored me anyways. At 15, she'd met a man who actually stayed. He was a good guy. He brought her back to life. We became a family, and I had finally outgrown my immaturity and anger. I liked him, he treated me like one of his own. He was a military guy, Navy, very disciplined. Strict but not mean. Stern but fair. Hated cursing. I would get beaten severely if I cussed, so I didn't. Mom did, and he'd hit her every time. When she started drinking again, it got worse.

"MOM! Just stop!" I would beg.

"Fuck that, I'm an adult!"

Smack!

When he'd had enough of her alcoholism, he left, and I went back into my shell. I became numb. She'd taken two people away from me and left me alone. I taught myself to never feel. I was scared of emotion, every emotion, happy, sad, mad, whatever. I stopped allowing myself to care about things, but it took practice. I killed our dog, choking it with its own leash, and threw it in the trash can. The killing calmed me down, but I knew I needed more as I watched the trash truck drive away with Scooby's corpse in the back. The next day, angry that my mom was drunk again, I put duct tape over our cat's face and locked it in my bedroom. I watched it struggle to live. I was calmed down as I watched it take its last breath. I carried it by the tail down to my mom's room and left it on her bed. She never mentioned it.

Killing things did for me what a Valium does for most people.

There were good times in life, too; it wasn't all gloom and doom. She would go months sober, and things would be normal, but she would ultimately fall back into her self-destructive ways.

She died when I was 18. I didn't kill her, but I didn't save her either. It was here, on this beach.

She liked to read with a glass of wine, down on the sand with her toes in the water. She had this inflatable unicorn flotation device that she would lie on for hours. I can't remember what she was wearing that day, but I'll never forget that the book she was reading was called Jack and Diane 4: Hang on to 16. Every time I hear that song, I think about her. At some point, she passed out, and the tide rolled in. The current swept her out to sea. I watched her go from the exact position I was sitting in now. Could I have saved her? Yes. Should I have? Probably, but I didn't.

I reported her missing the next morning, and the morning after that, her body washed up onshore 25 miles away.

I was snapped back to reality by laughter coming from the neighbors as they walked from the back of their house, across the sand, to the water. My wife looked back towards me and waved. I held up my forefinger and stood, satisfied with getting my emotions in check, ready to have a few drinks and meet this new girlfriend of Justin's.

I hurried through my house and met them down at the water.

"There he is!" They all turned to look at me. I stood stunned.

"Betty," my wife said, "this is my husband, Charles. Charles, this is Justin's girlfriend, Betty Griner."

Chapter 11: Tears for Fears

My brain was not ok with spending the evening with Officer Griner. A large, masculine woman, I gave her a fist bump instead of a handshake. She was loud and obnoxious. She constantly stroked her long dreads, showing them off, telling us how long they took to grow, and how everyone was always jealous because she had that good hair. They looked ridiculous to me, but even with that, it was her arrogance and attitude that made her unattractive. She had that 'God complex' police officers are always accused of having, and she made herself out to be the hero in all her stories. She tried to come off as some noble servant of the state. I had a hard time listening to her speak. Her vocabulary reminded me of a 17-year-old boy hanging out with his friends after football practice. F this, f that. She had so much anger and hate for the people she was sworn to protect, it just didn't make any sense. Both Dan and Dave wore looks of sheer embarrassment every time she opened her mouth. My wife was already drunk, so she didn't notice. She was so cute, just giggling the whole time. Justin, on the other hand, sat there like a love starved teenage girl, definitely the beta to his girlfriend's alpha.

The final straw came when she spoke about why she was on vacation. She bragged about shooting a thug, then being paid to take a week off.

Irritated, I asked her to explain.

"Well," she started, looking around at all of us as we sat around a bonfire on the beach, "we went to the YMCA to assist a detective in questioning a person of interest. I recognized the guy, I busted him before. I couldn't believe he was in charge of children. Anyways, he runs to his office as soon as he sees us. I think he was trying to erase whatever he had on his computer. I asked him to stop, and the guy goes nuts! We finally calm him down and take him outside, when he breaks free and starts running away. I didn't know that he had a gun on him, I thought my partner had already patted him down, so when the guy pulled it out, we shot him. There were kids out there, he could've hurt someone! I'm a hero, they're lucky I was there."

I tapped my wife's hand, then stood and walked back home without a word. They were all drunk, I doubt they even noticed.

I sat in the dark, alone, talking to myself, trying to keep my brain from going back and tearing that woman's head off in front of everyone.

My wife stumbled in, "Babe? You ok?"

"Yeah, I'm good," I said, "I know that lady. Justin's girlfriend is the one who murdered Director Douglas! I was there. She's lying about what happened! SHE'S LYING!"

My wife turned on a light and stared at me. I could see how drunk she was, and I smiled. I was happy that she was having a good time, even though I was irritated.

"Charles..." she spoke slowly with her eyes closed, "I think she was a boy! Ha ha ha." Her laugh humbled me. She was adorable. "I'm hot," she said, taking off her clothes.

I watched her, admiring how attractive she still was after all these years. My friends were right, I way outkicked the coverage. I wasn't mad anymore. How could I be with my angel standing here in front of me? She just saved Officer Griner's life without even knowing it.

"Come on." I grabbed her hand and led her to bed. She was snoring by the time I shut off the light.

The rhythm of her breathing while lying on my chest eased my brain. I stroked her head softly and counted my blessings. She was a perfect person, and me, I was not. I was a liar and an impostor. I was weak. I didn't deserve her. She shouldn't have to be burdened with my baggage. She deserved someone good, someone honest. Someone like... Director Douglas.

My brain woke up.

"Hero, Justin!" My wife mumbled in her sleep. It was her one annoying trait.

"What, babe?" I asked gently.

"His girlfriend is a hero."

I got out of bed angry. The director was a good man, and Griner was blatantly lying, disrespecting his name. I walked to the bathroom to splash some water on my face and cool myself down. I looked in the mirror, "Breathe... Relax." I took a few measured breaths and actually smiled when I heard my wife giggle in the other room. I wondered what she was dreaming about. "I'm back," I whispered, crawling back into bed.

"You're my hero," she mumbled, snuggling back into me.

"Thank you, baby." I kissed her on the forehead. "Go to sleep, love."

"Betty Griner is a hero."

"No, she's not, sweetie pie," I said, still petting her head.

"Uh-huh, she told me. She told all of us. She said she saved the children from that kid fucker!"

I walked through Dan and Dave's house, then easily made my way to Justin's room in the dark. I'd been there a thousand times. Using the spare key that they kept under a rock near the front door, access was easy. I walked into the bedroom, locked it, then stood, listening to them try to out snore each other. I could see their silhouettes, Griner's big body taking up most of the space, leaving Justin curled up in the corner.

72

I moved quickly, efficiently. I duct-taped Justin's mouth, bear-hugged him, and dragged him off the bed into the bathroom. I hog-tied him like a professional cowboy, using rope that I had stored in my garage. He woke up, but one well placed punch put him back to sleep.

Officer Griner never moved. By the time I was done duct taping her mouth and tying her arms and legs spread eagled to the columns of the 4 poster bed, she still hadn't shown any signs of life besides snoring.

I took a pillow and covered her face. The loss of air woke her up, and she started to struggle. I removed the pillow and lit a lighter, putting it close to her face so she could see me, but it was more so I could see her. The fear in her eyes was perfect. Gone was the obnoxious arrogance that was on full display earlier. Gone were the winks that came with the disrespectful and borderline racist jokes that she thought were so witty. All of that piss and vinegar was replaced with tears and fear.

"Do you want to shout? Shout! Let it all out!" I whispered. She couldn't get enough air through her nostrils, so I took my Charles keychain knife and cut a horizontal slit across the duct tape on her mouth, not caring if it cut her in the process. It did.

I put the pillow over her face and felt her scream in horror. I punched the pillow, hard, repeatedly, until she stopped. I removed the pillow and covered her mouth with my hand.

"Calm down!" I whispered angrily. I spread my fingers to allow her some air. I relit the lighter with my other hand. She bled from both her mouth and her nose.

"Do you know me?" I asked quietly. She nodded her head yes.

"Did you recognize me earlier?" She shook her head no.

"I was there at the Y. I saw what you did to that man. That was my friend. You and your cop friends murdered a good man."

She shook her head no again. I stabbed her under her chin, upwards through her jaw. She screamed a muffled scream through my fingers. I left the knife where it was.

"Shut up!" I demanded. I lit the lighter so she could see me. Her eyes were rolled up into her head. I touched the flame to her eyelash. That was a mistake, the smell of burnt hair made me gag. I spit up in her face, then put a fresh piece of tape over her mouth.

"You lied, you're a liar. Are you scared?"

I turned on a small table lamp. Her eyes darted from side to side, panicked. She was going insane.

"Hey, focus!" I slapped her. "HEY!"

She looked at me, tears flowed freely. I pulled out a large butcher knife and started cutting off her prized dreadlocks. I pulled her hair hard, cutting pieces of scalp along with them. She passed out. I slapped her back awake.

74

"I'm going to give you a chance to live. I'm going to ask you questions. If you answer them all correctly, you can go, if not, you die right here, right now. I'm going to stick this knife through your chest and twist."

As I spoke, I used the edge of the blade to cut a thin line from the corner of her burnt eye, down her face, to her neck, to the middle of her chest, then stopped with it pointed down above her heart.

"Are you ready?"

She shook her head no. I pushed down on the knife hard enough to hurt, but not cut. She whimpered as she nodded her head yes.

"Ok, here we go. Did you lie? Are you a liar? Was he guilty? Are you a bad cop? Are you scared? Do you want to die? Does this hurt? Do you remember his name? Did you murder him?" I rattled off my questions rapid fire. She shook her head yes, yes, no, yes, yes, no, yes, no, yes, then stopped, looking at me, wondering if she did it right. There was hope in her eyes. She raised her eyebrows, asking if she was right. She felt that she was correct, and the suffering would stop. I could hear her trying to say, "I did it. I did it right. Let me go... You said you would let me go..."

"Wrong!" I plunged the knife into her chest. "You didn't murder him, he was already dead by the time you shot. Your friends murdered him."

I waited until she died before getting up and grabbing Justin's still unconscious body so I could stuff him in the closet. I went into the bathroom and cleaned myself up. As I left and passed Officer Griner, I stopped, wondering why my brain thought it would be so funny to leave her with her mouth stuffed full of her dreadlocks. I thought it was overkill.

Dang it!

I saw my keychain knife still poking through her face and cursed myself for being so dumb. My brain wasn't satisfied, I had a thought right as I was about to leave.

Justin was technically a witness. I turned back and dragged him out of the closet, cut the rope from his feet, then wrapped it around his neck.

"Hey, Justin. Wake up!" I slapped him a few times until he opened his eyes.

"CHARLES!" I heard his muffled yell through the tape. He was confused. Every emotion flashed in his facial expressions as he tried to figure out exactly what was going on. I pulled him up to a standing position by the rope, then turned him around so he could see his dead girlfriend on the bed.

He screamed, and I squeezed the rope tighter.

"Charles, no, please. No. Stop! Why? Charles, it's me, Justin!" he mumbled.

I squeezed the rope until he stopped moving and his body went limp, then pushed him on top of Officer Betty Griner. I shut the light off and left.

When I got back home, I put my clothes in the laundry and climbed into bed feeling incomplete. I wasn't happy with my brain. Justin didn't have to die, that was cruel and unnecessary.

"Where were you? I had the craziest dream," my wife asked sleepily.

"I had to poop, you want a smell? I saved you some." I put my hand to her face, pretending that it was the hand I wiped myself with. "What was your dream about?"

I dreamt that you left me for that cop, Justin's girlfriend. I dreamt that I walked in on you, her, and Justin in bed together.

I didn't respond.

Beeeeep

My phone chirped, low battery. As I went to plug it in, I remembered that I was supposed to text Detective Lucas back. I had planned to send a 'what's up?' message and wait till morning to read his reply, but he'd already sent his message.

'Good news, we found Carla, and your HR lady, Evelyn, is alive!'

Chapter 12: Mayberry and Kitt

They say age is just a number, and it is, but it's a number that represents something. For instance, the sirens that woke me up that morning, when I was, say, 23, would've scared me and had me running and hiding, ducking and dodging, scared that they were going to catch me.

Now, the number 48 represents wisdom. A life's worth of experience has been a far greater teacher than any professor or book.

I've been going to Oceanside since I was young. I knew everyone, and everyone knew me. I also knew that this little Mayberry police department with their Barney Fife deputies would be running around in circles, clueless, for a long time after me and the wife left, which I was ready to do. My brain had other ideas.

"TODD!" I yelled from my front porch, "Hey Todd, wait up!" I jogged down the driveway to catch up with Sheriff Todd Marley, who was standing with his hands on his hips next to his police car, looking confused.

"Todd, what happened?" I asked. I saw Dan and Dave each sitting in the back of separate police cars, both crying, both with blood-stained shirts.

"I can't remember where I put my doggone hat! I just had it."
He scratched the top of his balding head. "I came out of the
house, then I went to..." He was talking to himself.

"No, Todd, what happened here? What's up with all this?" I
pointed at the house, the yellow tape, and the squad cars.
"What happened to Dan and Dave?"

"Murder suicide," he said absently, still focused on his hat.

"What?" I asked.

"Yeah, little Justin and his boyfriend. There was some freaky
stuff going on in there. I'm not the judge, so I'm not going to
judge, but there was some unnatural stuff going on inside
there." He finally turned to look at me.

"Oh, hey Charles!" He said it as if he were seeing me for the
first time. He smiled, shook my hand, then stood back,
rocking on his heels, thumbs in his belt loops. "Man, I
remember you when you were just a little guy chasing after
your mama, God rest her soul. How's the family? I didn't
know you were in town." He was genuinely happy to see me.

We didn't even talk about the murders. As we watched
investigators and detectives scurry around like a bunch of
ants, we talked about my kids, the weather, and his wife
having Alzheimer's. I told him I had planned to do some
fishing.

"I wish I could go with you, I'm too old for this," he said after
a moment of silence. "I should've been out five years ago."

"Ah, come on, age ain't nothing but a number. You're still getting around, you still look good. You probably forgot more than any of these yahoos ever knew," I said, pointing towards the house, "you're still winning."

"Father time is undefeated," he replied, looking at me.

"Is there anything I can do here to help?" I asked, "you want a drink? I have a fridge full of..."

"The refrigerator!" he said, smacking himself, interrupting me. "I set my hat on the fridge. I bent down to grab a bottle of water, it fell off, and I set it up there. Damnit! If my head wasn't attached..." He started to walk towards the house, shoulders slumped, kicking at the dirt.

"Hey, we're heading back today, see you next year?" I called after him.

He held up his arm and half waved, "Not if I can help it."

I wasn't a suspect. I took another look at Dan and Dave, who were both still sitting motionless, with the exact same shocked looks on their faces, then walked back to my place.

My wife met me on the porch.

"Murder suicide," I answered her unasked question. "Justin and his girlfriend."

"Justin? Why? Oh my God!" She started to cry. I gave her a hug and held her as she sobbed into my shoulder.

"I don't want to be here," I said for my own selfish reasons.

"No, we need to stay for Dan and Dave. Oh my God, they must be crushed. Babe, why? no..." She resisted until I said, "Too many memories."

The ride home was a lot different than the ride there. I drove. She sat silent, looking out the window.

We saw the gas station where I stole the keychain knife, and I felt a tinge of guilt that I took something that wasn't mine just to make my wife laugh. I felt bad that I gave in to peer pressure. I thought back to the last time I did that.

I was 21 and trying my best to fit in. I lived in a college town but wasn't enrolled in a school. I worked at a bar washing dishes and serving food on the main strip. I was a loner and would watch all these young, confident men and women with so much promise and potential come in and out every day. I was jealous, I wanted to be one of them. I wanted to hang out, get drunk, talk to all those gorgeous coeds, and just live that life.

I met a girl named Patty who used to come into the bar by herself. She was a little overweight and very shy, but she was nice to talk to, and I really liked her. She knew a few of the 'cool' girls from some of her classes, and I was introduced to that crowd. I was finally able to meet and hang out with the people I looked up to. I had low self-esteem and felt like I had nothing to offer, so I made it mostly by doing whatever they did, but I always did extra. If they took a shot, I took two. If they shotgunned a beer in 10 seconds, I did it in 5... Anything to prove my worth.

The alpha of the group was a guy named T-bone. He was loud and obnoxious, but good looking and funny. He accepted me as one of them and liked to call me Charlie Brown. I wore the name like a badge of honor.

It was all fun and games until T-Bone saw me talking and laughing with Patty. He made a big deal out of it, saying I was in love with a pig, and everyone else joined in. I was embarrassed when they asked if I was actually into her, and like a coward, I said I didn't. To make it worse, I started calling her the same names everyone else was calling her.

T-Bone called me a liar. He said that the only way to prove It was to have sex with her, then dump her. So I did.

It was nice, though. I really had a good time with Patty, she was a nice girl. We talked and laughed and joked. She was a good person and was easy to get along with.

The next night at the bar, after a round of them busting my chops about being a virgin, which I wasn't, I told everyone that me and Patty had sex. Big mistake! All the guys, and even some of the girls, acted like I had done something so egregious and grotesque that I could never live it down. Embarrassed, I said that I just did it as a prank, and when Patty walked into the bar, I called her a pig. I told her I had a thing for farm animals, and I didn't want to see her again. I said the whole thing was a big joke. She kept a brave face, but I could see the hurt in her eyes. She simply said "ok", looked away, then went and sat by herself. T-bone called me over and gave me a high five.

"You're a stud, Charlie Brown! Someone get him a drink! You're the man! You're the fucking man!"

I was finally 'the guy', and I felt great. I'd never been the guy before, and it was the cool kids who were calling me that!

This was a pivotal time in my life, too, because this was the first time that I realized that my brain had its own way of seeing things. While the rest of me was enjoying the free drinks, my brain was calling me a coward for giving in to peer pressure. While I was feeling good about having friends and fitting in, my brain wanted to kick my own butt.

At 2 am that night, when the bar closed and all my best friends were leaving, my boss asked me to stay behind and take out the trash, which I did without hesitation.

Cough cough cough!

I heard someone getting sick by the side of the building. I walked over to see who it was and if they needed any help. T-Bone was doubled over, throwing up.

"Charlie Brown! I'm good, I'm good. I think it was the fucking hamburger. I think I got food poisoning. Damnit, I'm good though." He stood up straight and took a deep breath. "Hey, I got beers at home, come on, let's keep drinking," he said, walking towards his car, a black Trans Am that looked just like the Knight Rider car, Kitt. I followed, excited that I'd been invited to hang out.

*"My keys!" he patted his pockets, "Fuck! They're right there!"
We could see them through the window on the floorboard.*

*"Wait, what year is this car? 85, right? I got a trick." I ran to
my car and grabbed some fishing line from my trunk. I jogged
back, then opened his car door using a trick I learned from an
old fisherman, then climbed into the passenger seat.*

*"Charlie Brown! You are the fucking man!" T-Bone yelled as
he started his car. "I can't believe it, man, you opened my
fucking car with a fishing line? Hell yeah! And you bagged
that pig... ha ha ha! That's what I can't believe. Ha ha! Yuck! I
can't believe you touched that bitch. Oh my God! Ha ha ha!"*

My brain skipped when he talked about Patty.

*"Let's go!" he said. He turned his head to make sure there
was no traffic, and when he did, I put the fishing line around
his neck and squeezed. Instinctively, his hands went to his
neck, and his foot pressed the gas pedal to the floor. The car
jumped forward, slamming into a vehicle parked just ahead
of us. I didn't let go. The nylon fishing line cut through the
young man's flesh easily, squirting blood across his
dashboard and windshield. It was over quick, but I didn't let
up until I felt the line stop, unable to cut through the spine.
His head fell unnaturally to the side, essentially decapitated.
T-Bone was deceased, but I was still amped up. I grabbed him
by the hair and repeatedly slammed his face against the
steering wheel, trying to disconnect his head from his body.*

Was it unnecessary since he was already dead? Yes. Did it
make me feel better about being so cruel to Patty? Actually,

no, but I vowed to never give in to peer pressure ever again, and I haven't until now, with my wife.

Beep beep… A text from Detective Lucas.

'Hey, are you still in Oceanside? You'll never guess what I just heard. Hit me back when you can.'

I looked at my wife and pulled off the exit.

She looked around, surprised, "Hey, where you going? What's going on?"

"I'm turning around. My conscience hurts. I can't live with myself knowing I stole from that store. I'm going back to pay."

Chapter 13: Honey hole

We didn't go back to the store, my wife asked me not to. She was physically and emotionally drained and just wanted to go home and sleep. I felt bad that it was partially my fault that she felt that way.

I'm glad we didn't return to the store. If those murder documentaries have taught me anything, it's that there is always an 'aha moment' where the killer gets caught and he realizes that he zigged where he should've zagged. Even viewers at home (who should be rooting for the cops, by the way) will yell at the screen, saying, "No, don't do that! Don't go there!" then sit in disbelief at the stupidity of the killer. They're left saying, "Aw man, nobody would be that dumb in real life!" Or the big one, "No wonder they got caught."

Luckily, my wife saved me from having such a moment, and instead, just made me promise not to steal again.

I dropped her off at home, got her settled in, then grabbed my fishing poles and headed to the lake. I still had a few days of vacation left.

I stopped at 7-11 for a 6-pack of Bud Light and finally returned the text to Detective Lucas, telling him I was back. I asked if he had a honey hole in response to his fishing question to me the first day we met.

'Yes, as a matter of fact, I do. When?' He replied immediately.

'Now.'

'Ok, I'll send the location!'

I exchanged the 6 pack for a 12, then sat and my car and waited for him to tell me where to go.

A homeless guy appeared at my window, begging, "Hey, can you buy me something to eat?"

"What do I get?" I asked, irritated. "Do my windows, I'll buy you a sandwich."

"Aww come on man, can't you just...?"

I rolled my window up, ending the conversation, not letting his laziness ruin my mood. I thought about killing him, but I just let it go. I killed a homeless guy before, cut his head off. It was my first decapitation.

It wasn't as spectacular as you'd think it would be. I thought it would be like the movies, where you cut off a man's head, then held it up victorious, with the look of horror permanently etched into his face. It wasn't like that at all for me. It was a lot of work. There was a lot of pulling and tugging. It was wet and messy. I spent half the time trying to cut through his spinal column.

I probably should've used a hatchet or a machete, instead of a kitchen knife, I don't know, it was all just a very unsatisfying experience. I ended up putting it in a Salvation Army donation bin... My brain thought it'd be funny.

The detective's honey hole location came through, and I immediately entered it into Google Maps, then followed the step-by-step directions.

"Wait a minute," I said to myself. I looked at my map again, "What the heck?" I was headed towards the exact spot where I left Carla. I slowed down, ignoring my instincts, allowing my brain to talk me into believing that it was just a coincidence that I'd pulled onto the exact same trail. It, was curious. I, was cautious.

There was movement to my left. I saw a trail I'd never noticed before with a vehicle driving down it. I checked my map, it directed me to follow its path. I moved my pistol from the passenger seat to my lap just in case it was some kind of ambush. My brain was confident that there was no way the detective could know what I'd done, but that was his job, and he said he'd been doing it for a long time, so he was obviously good at it.

I, however, did not share the same confidence. If I was caught, and it really looked like I was about to be, I wasn't going out without a fight. Somebody would die right then and there if they thought I was just going to be handcuffed and taken away. I continued on, ready for whatever.

"This way!" I heard him before I saw him. Detective Lucas was climbing out of his Ford F150. He pointed for me to pull up next to him.

Still leery, I did.

I got out and looked around, trying to act like I'd never been in the area. "This is your spot, huh?" I asked.

He walked over and greeted me with a handshake. "Yeah, you ever been here?"

"Nope."

He stared at me, hard.

"Never. You've never been out here?"

"No." I stared back, tense.

"I just figured..."

"Wait," I cut him off, "is this some type of interrogation? If you have something to say, say it."

"Grr! I'm sorry, man. Damnit! Remember I told you that I can't turn off the detective in me? I forgot how to just communicate like a normal person. I'm sorry, ha ha, I was just saying, it's so close to your work... I figured, maybe you, I don't know, snuck away at lunch, or came after work. I don't know, man, my bad, I apologize. I'm not Detective out here, I'm just Dewayne. Dewayne Lucas, nice to meet you." He extended his hand again, as if meeting for the first time.

I laughed and shook his hand. His apology was sincere. "It's all good, man, ha ha ha." I forgave him.

Visibly relieved, he turned and grabbed his gear from the bed of his pickup as I grabbed mine. He saw my beer and pulled out a cooler.

"Oh, I got adult beer," he said, opening it and showing it full of Coors Light.

"Urine flavored water, nice. Ok, I mean, you're obviously a connoisseur." We laughed, then started down the trail towards the water.

"I never actually fished here," he said, leading the way. "Hate to be morbid, but this is where they found your friend Carla. She was murdered here. Well, over there a hundred yards, but yeah. I came out here to investigate, and I thought about you."

"Someone is dead, murdered, and you thought about me?" I asked, half jokingly.

"No, ha ha, that came out bad. I meant, look around." He stopped at a clearing at the edge of the lake. It was the perfect spot. Large enough that you knew there were huge fish, but it was surrounded by trees, so it felt private. We were physically close to civilization, but it felt like we were miles away. Yes, I've been here before, many times.

We sat on a log, dropped our lines in the water, and opened the first of many beers. Conversation was easy and light until it wasn't. I told him about Regan's husband, Jhonny. I threw out the idea that maybe he found out about her affair and wanted to kill them all. Jhonny was a coworker who was known to have a bad attitude and a short temper. The detective and I ran through all of the different scenarios from the ridiculous to the plausible. He said he would check into it.

We spoke candidly about our lives, our loves, and our losses. I told him about my kids, my wife, and how losing my dad at a young age affected me. I kept my mom's story to myself.

He didn't speak much about his past, mostly just about his wife and young daughter. He was absolutely and positively in love with both of them. It was refreshing to hear an adult male speak about his family with as much passion and adulation as he did. He felt the same way about his as I did about mine. He wasn't like a lot of the guys I hung around with. He didn't speak about women as objects. He didn't want to sleep with the dozens of ladies who threw themselves at him every day on the job. His wife made him happy, and he had no intention of doing anything but returning the favor; he was honestly a good guy.

Finished with a successful fishing trip (I caught 5 more than he did), and an empty cooler, we were walking back when he asked me how I ended up as a factory worker, "You're obviously intelligent, it seems like you could be anything you want to be. How'd you end up there?"

"Life," I answered simply, then returned with a question of my own. "How'd you end up being a detective?"

"Death."

I waited for him to explain, but he didn't until he reached his truck and put his stuff away. It looked like he was having a hard time searching for the right words.

"When I was younger, my brother was killed, murdered. They never found the guy. There were no motives. The cops couldn't find anything, so they just treated it like it never happened."

He looked down at the ground as he spoke.

"But it did happen." He finally looked up, tears in his eyes. "And I was left with the most, like, just, emptiest feeling. I felt lost, incomplete. Nothing about it ever made sense to me. People don't just kill for no reason and just disappear. Somebody did it, and somebody needed to pay. I wanted to, well, I still want to make sure that no one ever has to go through what I went through. That's why I became a cop. That's why I became a detective. I am that link between the bad guy and the victim. If only to give people closure. That's what I do."

He took a breath and looked away. We stood in an uncomfortable silence.

Beeeep beeeep

My wife's ringtone. I grabbed my phone, and saw the text from Detective Lucas from the day before.

"Hey, babe. Yeah... Yeah... yep. Ok. Alright... ok. Love you too" I said to her, then put my phone away.

I turned back to him, "Honey-do list on my day off."

He laughed, "Is there ever a day off?"

"Oh, by the way, you never told me, what about Oceanside?" I asked.

"That's right!" he said excitedly, "Remember Griner?"

"Who?" I acted like I didn't know the name.

"Officer Griner. The one who shot your friend, the director. She was killed out there. Murder suicide. They asked me to go out there and try to provide some insight. I leave tomorrow."

"What the heck?" I feigned surprise. "No way!"

"Yeah, lovers' quarrel. Open and shut case. They only want me because of what happened at the Y."

"Go to Shameeka's soul food. Best food you'll ever eat. Ask for Meka, tell her I sent you."

"Will do, thanks," he said gratefully. We shook hands, ready to go our separate ways, and before he released my grip, he said, "He was nearly decapitated."

"What?" I asked, clueless.

"I saw the look in your eyes, you wanted to ask what happened. I appreciate your candor. My brother, when they found him, he was nearly decapitated. Whoever it was, tried to take his goddamn head off!"

"Oh my God!" I said, shocked.

"Those motherfuckers left him dead in the front seat of his fucking Trans Am!"

I didn't flinch.

Chapter 14: Dear John letter

The next couple of weeks were uneventful. Work, eat, sleep, repeat. My workdays were long and boring, and my nights were just me, the wife, and our 65-inch TV. We did go see the new Denzel movie, and went out for Taco Tuesday, but that wasn't anything special, we always did stuff like that.

At work, the talk was still about Evelyn, Carla, and her husband, John. We all knew Regan, who worked night shift, was pregnant with John's baby. Jhonny, Regan's husband, worked on the day shift. There were a lot of jokes being made about her. The most popular being, Regan was a whore, that's why she had a thing for johns.

Ha ha.

I made it a point to try and get to know Jhonny better for my own reasons. I really didn't like him, though. He was a loudmouth, racist, homophobic jerk. If the situation were different, I would stab him through the eye socket with a rusty railroad spike, but I needed him alive. For now.

I sent a text to Detective Lucas saying that Jhonny was a serious person of interest. To add to the urgency, I said that there was a rumor going around that he might be moving out of state. Police picked him up that evening.

I sat with Jhonny in the break room the next day and listened to him complain about the way he was treated at the police station. He said they grilled him about the murders. I added fuel to the fire, saying that I overheard upper management in the restroom, speaking to Detective Lucas about him being a person of interest regarding Evelyn.

"He specifically said the name Jhonny," I said, because of a very public disagreement with her in the main hallway at the plant.

"They said it could be considered motive. That's why you ran her off the road."

"Fuck that!" he slammed his fist on the table. "That wasn't a disagreement, they put me on the schedule. I was supposed to be off. It was my off day, my son's birthday! They can't just put you on the schedule when it's your off day. She said I had to work, or I'd be disciplined. That's crazy, right? I had a right to be mad. Fuck that. What would you do? Seriously. If it was you, what would you do?"

He was irate, causing a scene, and I loved it.

"I wouldn't stand for it. I wouldn't let someone drag my name through the mud. I can't even imagine getting locked up for something I didn't do. Then, losing my job because I missed work? No sir, wouldn't be me," I said.

He sat silent. I added one more jab. "Hey, how's your wife, by the way? I heard y'all are expecting... congratulations!" I said it cheerfully, like I was genuinely happy for them. Like I didn't know the truth. Was it a cruel and unnecessary dig? Yes. Did it do its intended job of antagonizing an already volatile situation? Yes, probably, but that remained to be seen.

I could see beads of sweat form on his forehead. If I had an Instagram filter, there would be steam coming from his ears, and his head would explode like one of those mind blown memes. He stood and walked away without another word. I might have just created a murderer. If nothing else, at least an active shooter. My brain was so pleased with itself.

I met with my friend, Dewayne Lucas, at our fishing spot after work for a few beers. He refused to drink my Bud Light. He had his own six pack of Dos Equis.

"What the hell is that?" I asked.

"Beer," he answered.

"No, obviously, but what kind?"

He showed it to me to read for myself. "2 x's?" I asked.

"What?" He looked at it like he didn't know what I was talking about. "No. Dos Equis! It says it right there." He showed it to me again.

"Yeah, 2 x's." I was messing with him; he didn't know Spanish.

"No!" he was getting irritated, "Dos Equis!" He said it like 'Dose Seckies'. "What are you asking? Why do you keep saying 2 x's? It says the name right here! Look!" He showed it to me again. "Leave my drink alone, I don't talk about your rainbow beer."

He reached out and squeezed the open can I was holding, causing it to spill everywhere, wasting it. "How's that, Dylan!"

We both busted out laughing. I finished what was left of it, then tossed the empty can in the back of his truck.

He patted his pockets, searching for something. "Where is, my, bottle opener?" He said as he looked around.

"Here." I passed him my Charles keychain knife. It had a built-in bottle opener on it.

He took it, but didn't use it, he just stared at it. There was a pregnant pause.

"Where'd you get this?" he asked suspiciously.

Right then, I didn't know if it was just an innocent question or if I heard an accusatory tone in his voice. Either way, something changed. The light, playful banter was gone. I also wasn't sure if I let the question hang, or if my brain did, but the question did hang as I looked at him.

"Where'd I get what?" I asked, adding to the length of time between the question and its answer.

"This. The knife." He finally opened his bottle with it, then handed it back to me.

"Oh. I don't know, I've had it forever," I lied, "why?"

We started to walk towards the lake.

"Well, you know how I went to Oceanside, right? When I was there, I was talking with some of the guys, and someone asked which way I drove in. I told him, then someone else asked if I'd heard about the gas station murder just outside of town."

Detective Lucas stopped talking to take a sip of his beer. I finished mine and opened another. I handed him the bottle opener again. "Just hold it till we're done," I said.

"Anyways," he continued, "they said it was a brutal murder. They said that whoever did it, killed with the same kind of rage as Justin did with Officer Griner."

"Wait," I interrupted, "you never told me, what did you think about the Officer Griner murder? How'd that go?"

I wanted to see where they were with that investigation.

"I never went in," He said matter-of-factly. "They seemed to have it all wrapped up and taken care of, open and shut. They didn't need me. The sheriff even apologized to me personally for wasting my time, saying that we could have done it over the phone." He opened another beer and took a long drink before he continued.

"Where was I? Oh, out of curiosity, I stopped by the little gas station on the way home and spoke to the shop owner. I asked him if he remembered anything else, aside from the murder, that day. He said the only thing that stuck out was that he was missing a keychain knife with the name Charles."

"Really?" I laughed, "ha ha, how? Why? In a store full of items, why that?"

Detective Lucas paused. "I thought the same thing. He said it was the last one in the store. He said he was planning on taking it home that night because his nephew was coming in town. That was going to be his birthday present. When the murder happened and all the cops came, the last thing he did that night before closing was go in to grab the keychain, and it was gone!"

He looked over at me.

"Am I a suspect?" I asked, half joking.

"That beer you're holding is suspect!" he said. We laughed for different reasons. I waited until the moment passed to ask, "Didn't they have cameras?"

"Yes, they do, but he erased the tape out of habit. It's been part of his everyday routine for 30 years at closing time. None of the cops who were there thought to ask for it, and he never gave it a second thought until I asked days later."

"The tape?" I asked, "he knows what century we're in, right? Does tape even exist anymore?"

He looked at me, expressionless. We finished our drinks in silence.

I disturbed the peace. "What'd you think about Jhonny?"

"Guilty!" he answered. "Guilty as hell!"

My brain cheered.

"I don't have proof, though. I need something more. I need..."

"Concrete evidence! And it's already past 48 hours. Ha ha ha!" I joked.

He smiled but didn't laugh.

"I heard your HR lady is getting better. Hopefully, she recovers enough to help us out. Till then, my captain wants me to keep an eye on your pal Jhonny."

My brain had an idea. I checked the time.

"Hey man, you hungry?" I asked.

"I could eat," Dewayne said agreeably.

"Good, I know a place, best hamburgers you ever had. Plus, the game is on," I said, picking up my stuff and walking back to our vehicles.

He followed me to a bar and grille not too far from my job, where a lot of the guys came after work to blow off steam and hang out after a long 12-hour shift.

We walked in and headed straight to the bar. I introduced my friend Dewayne to people that I've worked with for years, and bought a round of Fireball shots, enjoying the camaraderie that alcohol and sports often bring.

"ARE YOU FUCKING FOLLOWING ME?" We all turned to see an inebriated Jhonny walking towards us, staring daggers at Detective Lucas

My brain smiled, "Got 'em!"

Chapter 15: Scot, One T

"Is he talking to me?" Detective Lucas asked with a smile.

"Gotta be," I laughed as Jhonny approached.

He stood there angry, breathing harder than he needed to. Everyone within earshot stopped doing what they were doing and turned to look.

"I wasn't following you. I'm just here watching the game," my friend said calmly.

"You're not going to catch me, asshole. You can't catch nothing wrong!" Jhonny was having trouble putting sentences together. I heard what he was trying to say, but what he said and what he meant were two different things. He was trying to say, "you're not gonna catch me because I didn't do anything wrong."

"Come on, little guy, let's go. You want to take me in, come on, let's see if you can take me!" Jhonny slurred every other word.

Dewayne ignored him.

"COME ON! YOU WANT TO MESS WITH THE BIG DOGS, YOU GET THE HORNS!" he continued to mangle the English language.

"Hey man, I think you've had enough. Why don't you go home and sleep it off?" Detective Lucas said.

"I AM ASLEEP!" Jhonny yelled.

He reached for the detective, who, without looking, like he had eyes in the back of his head, turned, caught Jhonny's wrist, and had his arm twisted behind his back all in one smooth motion. It happened so perfectly that it looked choreographed.

"ENOUGH!" Detective Lucas commanded. "Stop!" He had full control of the much larger man. "Listen, go home to your pregnant wife. She's grieving. She just lost her boyfriend. Go comfort her!"

"Oooh shit!"

"Ha ha ha! You hear what he just said!"

"Drop the mic!"

The crowd inside the bar laughed and made jokes. Most of them had their phones out recording the whole scene. The look on Jhonny's face said it all. I actually felt bad for him. He'd been going through a lot these past few weeks, and I couldn't help but feel partially to blame.

"Ok." I stood up to intervene.

"Are you done?" Detective Lucas asked as Jhonny struggled. "Are you done!" he said again.

"Yeah," Jhonny finally conceded. He looked around the room at everyone laughing at him, it was pitiful.

Detective Lucas let him go. I threw money on the bar to pay my tab and helped the defeated man to the door, telling everyone that I'd get him home safely.

The ride to his house was silent except for the quiet whimpers of a broken man.

I pulled into his driveway and noticed a black Toyota Tundra with people in it, 2 houses down. He didn't see it, his eyes remained closed as I led him to his front door.

"I didn't do anything wrong, I swear! I didn't kill anyone, man. I'm not a killer," Jhonny mumbled, almost crying.

"You gonna be ok?" I asked, concerned.

"Yeah, I'm good. Regan's at work. I'm just gonna get some sleep." He stumbled over the threshold. "Hey!" He turned to face me and extended his hand. "Thank you, man. Really. Life fucking sucks."

I flinched at his choice of words, but still shook his hand and left.

Returning to my truck, I saw that he'd left his work gloves on the seat. "I'll just give them to him in the morning,' I thought to myself, too lazy to get back out and return them to him right then.

I knew whose truck was parked down the street. It belonged to one of our managers, a guy named Scot, one T. As I drove past, I saw Jhonny's wife, Regan, lean over from her position In the passenger seat to kiss Scot, then get out and walk to her house. I watched the black Tundra pull off in my rearview mirror.

What a whore, I thought to myself, she reminded me of my mom. I felt angry for Jhonny. I was mad at what she was doing to him, but I couldn't kill her because she was pregnant. Right? I've heard killing babies is wrong.

I killed a kid before. A little girl, maybe 7 or 8 years old. I didn't hate her or anything, she wasn't bad, I actually didn't even know her. I did it to save her from a terrible life and to teach people a lesson about watching your kids and cherishing every moment. Unfortunately, it didn't work out the way it should have.

It happened years ago when I lived in an apartment. I used to come home every day and see 4 young kids playing outside by themselves with no adult supervision. I would cringe seeing toddlers run barefoot through the parking lot, back and forth across the street. Angry, I would think 'where are the effin parents?' (pardon my French!). I never saw them. It was the same scenario every single day. I would try to be nice and say things like, 'Where are your shoes?' or 'Be careful around the cars, they drive fast,' but they didn't listen. I didn't want to say much more than that, for fear of being accused as a pedophile.

Aside from being run over by a distracted or exhausted driver who's simply coming home from work, I was worried that a bad guy with bad intentions was lying in wait, just looking for the perfect opportunity.

Something had to be done. One day after work, I offered the oldest one a dollar to take my trash out, which she did happily.

I watched as she struggled with the heavy bag, walk to the dumpster, followed by her 3 siblings. As she attempted to lift it high enough to get it fully into the trash receptacle, I went over and slit her throat in full view of the other three kids. Young, energetic blood squirted everywhere. To my surprise, it was different than adult blood. A brighter red, it shot out fantastically from the girl's innocent little body. This blood had promise, a future. There was happiness in the naiveté of this blood. There was absolute promise and joy wasted as it drained from the child onto the dirty ground.

The others, too young to communicate, stared at their dead sibling, then at me. There was no way to explain to them that I just did them a huge favor. I wiped my blade off on the shirt of the child standing closest to me, then walked away.

There were police and investigators, wanted posters and rallies, helicopters and news crews, the whole community was on edge.

3 weeks later, I came home from work to see 3 young kids playing by themselves with no adult supervision.

My brain remained undecided whether I should take Regan or not. It was the first time I'd had a moral dilemma. On one hand, technically, a seed isn't a baby. On the other hand, a living organism is alive. I was overthinking, confusing myself. Is killing a baby worse than killing an adult? They're both...

HONK! HONK!

A car honked at me, snapping me back to reality. I'd been stopped at a stoplight. I waved an apology, then stepped on the gas.

HOOOONK!

I was nearly t-boned by a black Toyota Tundra flying through the intersection.

Scot!

I turned to follow him. He drove erratically, but it was easy to keep up. My brain was going through all the different scenarios of what I was going to do to him when I finally caught him. I wanted to inflict as much pain as possible for Jhonny. Maybe shoot out his kneecap? Razor blade his eyelids? Ha ha, I was getting excited.

'I'm gonna do it for Jhonny!' I did a Matt Dillon impression from the old school movie, The Outsiders, "We do it for Jhonny, man. Ha ha, I could see a young, pre-Karate Kid, Ralph Macchio, lying in the hospital bed. I laughed to myself for even remembering that old flick. I was always impressed that my brain was able to recall things like…

SMASH! CRASH!

My chest exploded in pain, as my seat belt tore into my pectoral and abdominal muscles. My head jerked forward violently. Whiplash sent an electric shock through my body, all the way down to my toes.

I'd been rear-ended. My airbag didn't deploy, and I was instantly filled with a murderous rage directed at the automakers who made this faulty safety device.

Where was Scot? I got out and looked around. The black Tundra was gone.

I thought about the passengers in the other vehicle, ironically hoping that no children were hurt. Thankfully, there weren't.

My brain took over and allowed every morsel of physical pain to turn into an anger that was magnified at every individual nerve ending in my body. The moments that followed were more like flashes of memory, as opposed to a single, continuous scene.

Flash! I grabbed a Covid mask from my glovebox that's been there since the pandemic, then got out. Their vehicle, totaled. Mine, barely a scratch. 'Just married' was written across their rear window.

Flash! Newlyweds, still dressed in their tux and gown. His pants unbuttoned, her top pulled down. They were starting the honeymoon early.

Flash! Blood everywhere, especially hers, in the passenger seat. Her body flinched randomly. It looked like her neck was broken by the way it hung down unnaturally; she never looked up. Her barely audible moans sounded painful over ragged breaths.

Flash! Her fingers grabbed for him as I ripped him violently through the broken driver's side window. "Babe..." she pleaded.

Flash! I stabbed him angrily, repeatedly. Rage-fueled aggression tore through the groom's chest as he died for another man's sins. I mutilated his upper torso with a piece of metal that I pulled from their car's mangled radiator housing.

Flash! I reached for my keychain knife, forgetting that Detective Lucas never returned it, so I used that same piece of metal to cut off the man's ring finger, then carelessly tossed it through the window at the wife. It landed in her lap.

Flash! The man coughed up blood and gasped for air like he was drowning, trying to stay alive. I went to my vehicle and grabbed a can of gasoline. I emptied the 5 gallons of unleaded over him, pouring some of it in his vehicle, splashing it on the lovely bride.

Flash! The flame was like a monster that swallowed the man whole. I spared the widow, my gift to the happy couple's family, then returned to my truck. I saw Jhonny's gloves still sitting on the passenger seat and tossed them in the fire, on top of the burning man as I drove away.

I felt better. Did I have to cut the man's ring finger off? Probably not. And was the fire just cruel and unnecessary? Yes. The real question was, did it fill that space in my being that could only be filled by anger and violence? Actually, no, it didn't. I wanted Scot, but Bridget and Ted, the newlyweds, got in the way.

45 minutes later.

BEEP BEEP BEEP... A text from Dewayne, 'Good news, Evelyn's awake!'

I ignored the text, thinking I'd get back to him the next day, as I was 2 miles from home. I wasn't concerned with Evil Lyn. I destroyed her face! She was years from ever communicating again.

Ring, ring ring... A call from Detective Lucas.

Annoyed, I answered, "What's up, man?"

"Hey! He did it again!" he said excitedly.

"Who did what?"

"Jhonny just killed again. We got it. Hardcore proof! We're going to get him now!"

"What?" I didn't understand what was happening.

"It's over, we got proof. There was a murder. He tried to get rid of the evidence by burning it. It didn't burn. Ha ha ha! He tried to burn the gloves he wore, but they didn't burn! He had his name on the gloves! Ha ha ha! You can't make this stuff up!"

Ha. Actually, you can.

Chapter 16: Nachos Bell Grande

I let Detective Lucas talk me into meeting him and his officers at Jhonny's house. He said he'd appreciate my help as the go-between, especially since I just drove him from the bar.

I agreed to talk to him on behalf of the police if things went sideways. I was only there to support 'a friend.'

I changed clothes in a gas station parking lot, then pulled onto the same street that I was just on a little while ago. I came in from one direction, at the same time that a squadron of squad cars came in from the other. A few drove past me to drive up the alleyway and cover the back of the residence. I saw the black Toyota Tundra, which didn't make any sense.

"Why is Scot here?" I wondered. I got out of my car cautiously, just as Detective Lucas got out of his. He walked over and greeted me with a handshake and a bro hug. I could smell the alcohol from earlier at the bar all over him. I reached into my glove box and pulled out a small can of Axe body spray that one of my sons left in there a long time ago.

"You been drinking, officer?" I joked as he sprayed himself.

"You should talk, did you miss the hole in your gas tank? Put some hair around it. Remind me not to light a match!" he said half jokingly.

I never had the chance to wash up after the newlyweds.

"Hey, see that truck over there?" I changed the subject. "That's one of Regan's boyfriends, I know that truck."

"Jesus. How many men does this bitch have?"

I noticed his interesting choice of words as he went on to explain that there were already police coming to this address for an earlier domestic violence call. He popped a piece of gum into his mouth, then offered me one. I declined.

"Wait here," he said, "but call my phone, I'll put it on speaker so you can hear what's going on."

I did as he instructed, then watched him walk up to the front door with five other uniformed officers. I still felt like something was off, I just couldn't place it. Detective Lucas knocked on the door, then waited. He knocked again, no answer. When he looked back at me, I just shrugged my shoulders.

Detective Lucas nodded to the officer standing next to him, then stood to the side. The officer stepped to the door and banged on it in that special way only police seem to know how to do.

"POLICE! OPEN UP!" He banged again. "OPEN UP, WE'RE COMING IN!"

A different officer armed with pump pump-action shotgun stepped over and pointed his weapon at the door handle just as it opened. Scot walked out apologetically with his hands up.

"Sorry! I'm sorry! I was coming! I thought it was my wife at first. I thought she followed me. I was hiding. I'm sorry. Oh my God, don't tell her, please. Is this being recorded? Can you stop the recording? Please! I was only here cuz she called. Her husband is crazy! He beat her up, grabbed his gun, and left. He told her he was going to kill a motherfucker's family for fucking with him. It wasn't me! I was getting nachos. From Taco Bell. Nachos Bell Grande!"

"Wait a minute! What?" Detective Lucas held up his hand.

"What, what? Which part? The nachos? Oh, I like the bell grande because they add the meat and the beans. I'm not a fan of the onions, so I tell them not to…"

"NO! Goddamn it! Jhonny! Where the fuck is Jhonny?" Detective Lucas was losing his patience.

"Jhonny? Oh, I don't know, she said he left. He took his pistol, got in her car, and left."

That was it! Her car was missing. If she was here, that meant Jhonny had her car.

Detective Lucas looked back at me again. I didn't have an answer.

Regan came to the door, battered and bruised. I heard the conversation.

Detective Lucas: Hello, Miss Regan. Are you ok? Who did this? Jhonny? Is he here?

Regan: No (starts crying)

Detective Lucas: Do you know where he went?

Regan: (shakes her head no)

Detective Lucas: Did he do this to you?

Regan: (Nods her head yes)

Detective Lucas: (looks at his watch) What happened exactly? I need you to tell me everything.

(He yells for paramedics to come check on her injuries.)

Regan: I came home early from work. He was passed out on the floor, drunk. I woke him up to tell him to go to bed. He was so mad. He said everyone was laughing at him because of me. He said he was gonna kill everyone who was there, except Charles Brown. He said everyone made fun of him, he was humiliated, and he didn't even do anything wrong. He kept talking about Charles being his only friend. And Charles being the only real person. Charles this, Charles that, blah, blah, blah. He was crying like a bitch and I told him so. That's when he called me a whore and started hitting me. He said he was going to murder the detective and everyone in the bar. I asked him why he hit me. He just looked at me and said it was a good night for a murder suicide. He took his gun and left. I called 911... what took you guys so long to get here? I could be dead already. Me and my baby.

Detective Lucas: Did he say where he was going?

Regan: I JUST TOLD YOU WHAT HE SAID! I didn't know what to do, so I called Scot. He was at Taco Bell getting nachos...

Scot: See! That's what I said! Nachos Bell Grande! Without the onions, right, babe? I don't like...

Regan: (shoots Scot a death stare)

Detective Lucas: (stands up to leave) Ok. (He looks at the officer standing next to him.) Get her info, put an APB out on the car. (He turns and stares at Scot) I don't believe you.

Scot: What? Why?

Detective Lucas: (To the officer) Take him in for questioning. Call his wife and let her know everything. She can decide if she wants to get him out. I'll be in touch.

I saw the detective walk from the house towards me with an irritated look on his face, followed by a crying Scot yelling,

113

"NO! DON'T CALL HER! PLEASE! DETECTIVE, PLEASE, NO! Oh my God! Casey is going to be so mad!"

I was a little upset that I'd have to wait to get to Scot. My plan to put his head in a vice and drill thirty 1 mm holes through his skull was put on pause. At least for now. Too bad, too, because I could already hear it. It would be like everyone's worst fear when going to the dentist.

"He was drunk, right? When you dropped him off?" Detective Lucas asked.

"Way past wasted," I said matter-of-factly.

"Did he have any enemies that you knew of?"

"Besides you?" I answered sarcastically, then added, "Let me text him."

We leaned against my car as I typed, 'Hey, where you at?' Then stood and watched the scene as it unfolded in front of us. I couldn't take my eyes off of Scot crying in the back of a police car. Regan looked like she was flirting with a paramedic.

"He respond yet?" the detective asked impatiently.

Ring Ring Ring

I thought it was my phone ringing at first, but it was his.

"Hello? What? Wait a minute, what?" He looked at his screen in disbelief. "You are what? Listen you motherfucker... NO! YOU LISTEN TO ME!" He was losing his cool, visibly shaken.

I didn't know what was happening or how I could help my friend. "Take a breath," I said calmly.

He nodded, inhaled deeply, then exhaled. "Where? On my way!" Detective Lucas put his phone in his pocket and ran to his car.

I jogged after him, "Hey! What happened?".

"He's got Keisha and Karma!"

I stopped and stared at him while he got in his car.

"Your friend Jhonny has my wife and daughter!"

Chapter 17: Shits and giggles Part 1

I've spent the majority of my life being the peaceful one. I do my best to avoid conflict. I absolutely hate confrontation, and I've been called all kinds of names for my unwillingness to fight. Of course, there are times when I had to, but I used every resource available not to. My dad hated that trait in me. My mom used to call me daughter sometimes. My wife used to call me weak.

I watched Detective Lucas speed off. Somehow, I was taken back to the day when my dad sped off.

I remember watching from my window. I heard yelling. I saw my mom stumbling up the driveway. I heard the squealing of the tires, then the skidding and smashing of the car.

I ran outside barefoot, in the dark, scared that a wolf or coyote would eat me. If not that, a vampire would swoop down and suck my blood. My imagination took advantage of my young mind.

I passed my mom, who managed to slur the word 'Hey', and kept going. I saw his car wrapped around a tree.

I ran up and saw him twisted and broken, bleeding and suffering, trying to live.

"Dad!" I was scared.

"Don't just stand there, damnit, go get help!" He demanded.

I started to leave when he said, "Not your alcoholic mom. She's drunk. She's worthless. Call the ambulance."

I didn't respond. I started to go again.

"Hey!"

I stopped and turned to listen, obviously not knowing at that point that these would be his final words.

"Boy, listen." He spoke through measured breaths. "My intentions were always good. My execution might have been bad, but my intentions were good. I'm sorry that I didn't say I love you enough, but I do." He reached for me, I pulled away.

"Do good," he said. "There will be times in life when you don't know what to do, and the answer will always be, do good."

I started to leave again.

"Hey!" He called out. I couldn't have known at that young age that he was stalling. He didn't want me to go. He was scared to die alone.

"I'm in pain," he said. "Help me. End it."

I sat, frozen, staring at my father.

"There's a pistol in the glove box. The 45. The one we shot the cat with, remember? Ha ha. Get it. Help me." His voice was different. It sounded weird to me, foreign. For the first time in my life, he sounded... weak.

I sat, frozen, staring at my father.

"Help me, son," he pleaded. He reached for me again. I pulled away.

"DAMNIT BOY! QUIT BEING THE LITTLE BITCH YOU ARE AND GRAB THE FUCKING GUN! PUT ME OUT OF MY MISERY! LET ME GO, GODDAMNIT, SET ME FREE!"

I didn't.

I just sat there, staring at my father as he died.

I didn't cry that day, but I do remember it as the day that I stopped feeling. I had become comfortably numb. Like the song on The Wall album. Looking back, my father's death was probably the first brick.

117

I didn't want to follow Detective Lucas, but my brain did. I wanted to stay away from the inevitable drama. I wanted to go home, get in bed with my wife, and dream about apricots and unicorns. Maybe I could even get a back rub. I should've stayed home that night my dad left us; maybe life would've been different.

My brain said, "Hey, let's go with the detective."

"NO!"

"Come on... Let's just go for shits and giggles. If nothing's happening, we'll leave." It was like the single friend trying to get the married friend to go out to the club.

"No," I said, even as I turned left when Dewayne's Ford F150 ahead of me turned left.

Chapter 17: Shits and giggles Part 2

Beep beep beep! A text from the detective, *'He's at the cliffs!'*

I knew where that was. It was only a few miles from our honey hole, which was in the same area that they found Carla. I couldn't shake the feeling that something bad was going to happen.

The cliffs were a wall of sheer rock 100 feet above a rocky shoreline. It was high enough to be exciting, but with common sense wouldn't be considered dangerous. People were there all the time, picnicking, reading, or just spending time with a loved one. It boasted a beautiful view of the lake and the surrounding area.

Detective Lucas said murder suicide, but I couldn't picture Jhonny doing that. It's just not how it works, nobody announces their going to do that before they do it.

I was stopped at a red light and lost him. I listened for sirens but curiously didn't hear any. Surely the detective called for backup, right?

I should've just gone home. Something just didn't feel right. My brain told me to continue, and as usual, I listened.

There were two ways to get to the cliff. I went to the entrance that was further away to drive to, but would be closer once I parked. I figured Detective Lucas would go to the other one since it was the more immediate route.

I pulled into an empty parking area and grabbed my pistol. I didn't have to check if she was loaded, I knew she was, she's never empty.

I thought about grabbing an extra magazine, just in case there was a shootout or something unexpected happened. I was stalling. I thought about the last couple of weeks and how sloppy I'd become in the execution of my executions.

Ha. I should trademark that, I thought.

"Ok, go help your friend," I said to myself.

I moved quickly on the gravel trail, trying to be quiet, unsure of what situation I was walking into.

"I DIDN'T DO ANYTHING THOUGH!"

I instinctively ducked behind a tree. It was Jhonny's drunk voice pleading. I moved silently into a position where I could see what was happening.

I saw Detective Lucas pointing a gun at Jhonny, who was sitting with the detective's wife and young daughter dangerously close to the edge of the cliff. Their legs hung over the side with nothing but jagged rocks below. Jhonny had his gun pointed at Karma, the detective's daughter.

"PUT THE FUCKIN GUN DOWN!" Detective Lucas demanded.

"This is your fault, detective. I told you over and over and over. I didn't do anything! You forced this." Jhonny nudged the child's head with his gun.

"Put the gun down. Back away from the edge," the detective said again. "You think you're so smart, don't you? We know about the newlyweds you killed tonight, Jhonny. We have your gloves."

"What? What newlyweds? What gloves? I was with you at the bar. Then I was at your home, with these two. There were no newlyweds! What are you talking about!" Jhonny sounded like a broken man. He sounded like he'd given up. Like the stress had beaten him down to the point where piling on more didn't matter, he couldn't go any lower.

Detective Lucas paused, as if in thought.

"Did you hear them laugh at me? Do you know what you're putting me through? I didn't do anything. I didn't kill John, I was already at work when him and Miss Carla were killed, I was already clocked in, I told you that. You checked our time sheets, right? And I couldn't have killed Evelyn either. Again, I was at work. I stayed late in the computer lab finishing my safety training. I told you all of this, but you still keep on. You're killing me, detective, so I'm killing them. You wanted me to be a murderer, well, here I am."

I had been creeping up to the cliff the whole time they were talking. I wasn't sure if Detective Lucas saw me, but Jhonny definitely did not.

"This is it!" Jhonny said, standing up. "Get up! Both of you!" he yelled at the girls, who did as he commanded.

Keisha looked over at her husband and was greeted with a smack to the face from Jhonny's gun.

"I told you not to look at him!"

"GODDAMNIT! STOP! OK! Ok, I'll back up and put my gun down. See? Look, I'm no threat. If you're gonna do this, take me. Let them go." Detective Lucas begged.

"No. Nope. Nobody loves you. You are weak and worthless. She's not the whore, you're just the loser!" Jhonny wasn't talking to Detective Lucas anymore, he was talking to himself. He'd finally lost it.

I paused.

Detective Lucas tried a different approach. "Hey. Hey man. Listen. I've been there. My first wife... wow! I could tell you some stories. I understand where you're at, trust me. Whaddya say, for shits and giggles, we just go somewhere, share war stories. I actually believe you. You convinced me. Whaddya say, man?"

"Everybody hates you, everybody laughs at you," Jhonny was still talking to himself, "She's a whore. Mama told you not to marry her. She said they would laugh. Now you have no friends. Except... except... Hey, Charles!"

He turned and smiled, surprised and genuinely happy to see me. His whole demeanor changed as if my presence offered some relief. He just knew I was there to save him from doing something he didn't really want to do, and he was thankful to have someone share his burden. The weight of the world had proven to be too heavy, but with a friend to help carry some of the load...

POP!

The single round from my .45 caliber pistol exploded through the back of his head effortlessly, and he fell to the ground. I used my foot to nudge his lifeless body over the edge of the cliff, then turned to look at Detective Lucas. I was a hero! Did I have to shoot him? No. And was kicking his body over the edge overkill? Yes. But I was the hero, so none of that mattered.

My friend Dewayne's face wore a look of shock, which was quickly replaced by relief that his family was safe.

Surprisingly, he did have a walkie-talkie, which he finally pulled out and called base.

"Go ahead, Detective Lucas."

"Janet, we caught him. Send everyone to the bottom of the cliffs by Lakeside Tower. My family's safe, I'll be in later with my statement," he said.

"10-4, detective. Good job. Glad to hear everyone's safe."

I allowed his family to shower me with praise for saving their lives. We could see the red and blues of the police in the distance, but couldn't hear the sirens since we were so far up.

Dewayne grabbed me by the shoulder, looked me in the eye, and shook my hand.

"Thank you. Seriously, man, thank you," he said sincerely. "I really appre…"

"Detective Lucas, do you copy?" The voice he called Janet came over his walkie-talkie. "I have the info from forensics you requested. I just found it, it was stuck in our spam folder for hours. I'm so sorry."

"Just give it to me," he said angrily.

"Sorry, detective. Anyways, they finally cleaned up the video and found the license plate of the vehicle from the church. It was registered to a Patricia Brown.

I stopped talking to Keisha to listen.

"It shows that we got the DNA from the knife. Also, the HR lady, Evelyn, was able to identify her attacker, and it was the same person, Charles Brown."

How? I wondered. My brain spoke up; she couldn't talk, but she could still write.

Detective Lucas flexed his jaw, "Copy." Without looking at me, I saw his hand twitch as he reached for his cuffs and tried to do the same maneuver on me as he did on Johnny at the bar.

I am not a broken, intoxicated man, though. My counter to his move ended up with the handcuffs on the ground, my arm around his wife's neck, and my pistol pressed firmly into the side of her temple.

Unfortunately, his pistol was aimed directly at my brain. I looked at him, distraught that my friend would betray me like he did.

"You had my Charles keychain knife analyzed?" I asked sadly. "I thought we were friends. I just saved your family."

"I told you I couldn't turn the detective off. Remember when I asked you about your hr lady? You told me that you heard that someone bashed her face. Nobody knew that at the time, we hadn't told anyone, my spidey senses started tingling."

I was mad at my brain for being so careless.

"Put the gun down, Detective Lucas. Back off, or honey here's dead," I said. "Now!"

I hit his daughter on the top of her head with the gun. Not as hard as I could've, just enough to get everyone's attention. The child started to cry. "Make her stop!" I commanded Keisha.

"She's hurt, asshole! That's what kids do when they're hurt," she tried to say, before I cut her off with a harder than necessary hit on the side of her head.

"STOP!" Detective Lucas said, putting his gun on the ground. "Stop, ok? Just let them go. We already caught our killer," he motioned at the cliffs, "and he's dead now. So let the girls go, I'll let you go."

"What! Hell no! Pick up your gun, shoot this muthafucka, Dewayne! You see what he just did! Hell no!" Keisha yelled. "Shoot this muthafucka!"

I flinched.

"Everyone just calm down," the detective said.

I was running out of time. Surely the police heard the gunshot, I had to go. I began to drag the woman back the way I came.

"NO!" She began to fight me. I hit her again. "Fuck you!" she said.

I flinched.

"Dewayne! Be a man! Be a full grown man for once in your life! Shoot. His. Ass!" She bled from her injuries.

"Babe, please, I got it. Just calm down," Detective Lucas pleaded.

"You got it? You got what? You still got your mamas tit in your mouth. Grow up you little bitch! Shoot this asshole!"

For half a second, I almost felt bad for him. I could tell that she didn't make his life easy. Even though he did the ultimate betrayal to me, I still considered him a friend and wanted the best for him.

"Let me go! Fuck you!"

I flinched.

POP!

Her head exploded in my arms. I let her go and grabbed the child before the detective could reach for his gun.

Yuck! I got blood in my mouth. As I spat and began to gag, Detective Lucas made his move, lunging for his gun.

POP!

I shot at the ground next to him, I didn't want to hurt my former friend. That was three shots. The cops would be coming.

Dewayne lay frozen on the ground. With a handful of Karma's hair, I dragged her with my left hand, while I pummeled her father with the gun in my right.

"Get up!" I demanded of him while putting the gun to her head. "If you really believe I'm a killer, then you know killing her means nothing to me."

"Please, Charles..." he had his hands up.

"Get the handcuffs." He did. "Take 20 steps that way and cuff yourself to that big tree." He did. I followed, then, after making sure he couldn't get loose, I emptied his pockets.

"If you yell, she gets it! I'll let her go when I get to the end of the trail and start my truck." I grabbed his pistol and his walkie-talkie talkie then dragged the little girl down the hill.

"Oh, by the way," I stopped quickly and walked back to where I left him. I bent down and put my face uncomfortably close to his, and stared into his eyes. "I was shocked by the way your brother T-Bone squealed like a girl when I tried to take his head off. It was unexpected, and I walked away disappointed. He lost a lot of respect from me that day."

I stayed a second longer to absorb the changing emotions that flashed across the detective's face before I dragged the little girl away by her hair.

"She'll be at the bottom of the hill!" I called out.

I kept that promise as I drove away casually. There were no police coming anytime soon. I knew because I had the walkie talkie turned on as I drove.

I called my wife. She picked up on the first ring, "Hey babe," she said sweetly.

I was choked up, emotional. I waited a full 30 seconds before finally managing a drawn out, "umm..."

"Aw, babe..." She knew. After a heavy exhale, she finally said, "Ok, I'll pack. How much time do I have?"

"I'm a half hour out," I answered.

She hung up without another word. She was upset. She liked our life here, she didn't want to move again.

Chapter 18: Peppermint Patty

Change isn't always good. Sometimes things are exactly as they should be.

I'd promised her that the last time would be the last time. She hated relocating, and every time we moved, it was further and further away from the kids. I know it was my fault; I got sloppy. I let the emotions of a personal bond get in the way. I slipped. At this point, I wondered if my brain was actually trying to set me up. Did it want me to stop? Why would it want me to get caught?

She met me at the door with my go bag and 3 suitcases full of our stuff.

"I'm sorry," was all I could manage to say. I could see the hurt in her eyes. She simply said 'ok', looked away, then went and sat in the passenger seat, waiting for me to change her life once again.

The drive out of town was quiet. And sad. There was no time to say our goodbyes to any of the people we called our friends. We stopped at our neighborhood convenience store to get gas.

"Do you want some peppermints?" I asked as I got out. She didn't answer.

"Babe?"

No answer.

"Patty!"

"What. Charles."

"Do you want some peppermints?" I asked again.

She was angry. Livid. She just sat, staring out the window. I knew what she was feeling, heck, I felt it too. I didn't want to move away, I liked my life. I enjoyed my job and my work friends.

I didn't have to speak or offer any explanation for why we were moving again, she already knew. She knew exactly who I was. She'd known ever since I took T-Bone way back in the day.

The day after I killed him and hurt her feelings at the bar, I went and found her to apologize for my weak and cowardly actions. I apologized for not standing up for her and letting my own insecurities play a part in some male ego pissing contest. Part of my apology was the confession to what I'd done to T-Bone. Surprisingly, she wasn't mad or upset at what I'd done, she was flattered. She called it romantic in a Greek tragedy type of way. No one had ever shown her that type of affection.

She was admittedly hesitant in the early stages of our relationship, but grew to learn that I would never do anything to hurt her, in fact, the opposite. If anything, I was overprotective. During one of our patented, 'just past buzzed talks,' she told me about the abuse she and her siblings went through. I sat in silence as she described the horror and shame they'd experienced. When she was done, I stood and gave her a long hug. "Let's go," I said.

We rode silently to her childhood home. Her literal house of horrors was in a rural county, not too far from the bar where we met. She watched as I walked into her father's bedroom and attacked the man in the exact same bed where most of the abuse had happened.

Two punches to the face confused him. I clumsily bound both his arms and legs, (I wasn't as efficient with hog tying grown men back then) then slit both distal tendons, which is the part that connects the bicep to the elbow. I also cut both Achilles rendering him immobile. I straddled him as he screamed and begged his daughter for help. She wore a sick look of amusement but did nothing. Tired of the noise, I stuffed a blood-soaked pillowcase in his mouth.

"Stop resisting!" I demanded. When he didn't stop, I used both fists to deliver a hammering blow to his midsection. "Stop resisting," I demanded again. He was trying to speak. "What?" I asked, removing the gag.

"I'm not resisting. Please!" I hit him again. He vomited blood. "PLEEEAASE!"

"Apologize," I said.

"I'm sorry. I'm sorry, man! I'm sorry!" he cried

"NOT TO ME! TO HER!" He hesitated, I hit him again.

"I'm sorry. I'm sorry. I was sick. I'm sick. I'm sorry, baby. Fuck!"

I flinched.

I actually believed him, but I still took my knife and stabbed him in the groin.

"AAAHHHH!" he screamed. I replaced the gag and stabbed him again.

I pulled my knife out of him, then turned and held it out to my future wife, Patricia. She stared at it, unmoving.

She looked at me, then the knife, then at him with a maniac's grin. I stood still and waited patiently. He shook his head no, begging and pleading, falling into the insanity that the pain brought.

Seconds clicked past. I made another dramatic motion, pushing the weapon towards her. She took it and moved slowly around the bed. He screamed into the bloody gag. I pulled it out of his mouth.

"Baby, please! No. Help me. No." He moved, and I hit him, knocking the wind out of him. He gasped for air. "Please, help your papa, sweet girl." That did it.

She stabbed him in the groin, then looked at me, excitedly, as if asking for my approval. I nodded, she did it again. Then again. Again and again, over and over, until her arms finally tired. She mutilated her father's genitalia and lower half in a gruesome display of retribution. Crying, she walked away, leaving me standing at the end of the bed. There was a bottle of vodka sitting on the nightstand that I grabbed, poured out over the body, then smashed it on his head.

Was stabbing him, then leaving the broken bottle sticking out of his chest, overkill? Yes. Did he deserve it for what he did to children? Also yes.

She would tell me years later how exhilarating it was, but how she would've done things a lot differently. It was an open ended statement, she never explained how or what she would've changed.

We bounced from motel to motel for almost a year before finally settling into something permanent. We found jobs and continued down our predetermined life course. I found a new honey hole... things were getting back to normal.

I made a fake Facebook profile to keep up with folks from my previous job.

Scot left his wife, Casey, to be with Regan full time. She gave birth to twins, and to nobody's surprise, Scot was not the father. Neither was Jhonny. Fittingly, it just said John Doe on the birth certificate.

Detective Lucas became famous for stopping a serial killer while losing his wife in the pursuit of justice. He quit the force, and the 48 hours show to become an independent consultant to law enforcement agencies around the country. He was always on TV advertising himself as a good guy who is in the pursuit of two things, justice and the perfect honey hole. Personally, I think he was searching for me. I think he wanted to deal with me himself. He never mentioned my name publicly.

Everything was going just fine for me, life was good. Not so much for my wife. She didn't like our new place, she didn't have friends, and she hated her job.

Her normally happy face became resting b-word face. (Pardon my French.) Gone was the happy-go-lucky charm and the small town, good natured cheer, replaced by sharp tongued sarcasm, quick anger, and mean spirited put downs.

It all came to a head after we had a decent night drinking at an out of the way bar and grille. I was too drunk to drive my truck, so my job was to play the in-car DJ from the passenger seat.

Calling her a cautious driver is me being generous to my wife. Nervous is a better word... She just drove too slow. Cars beeped and passed us, which was no big deal, it always happened, but one guy kept flashing his high beams, yelling out his window, and tailgating us. Enraged, she slammed on the brakes, causing him to run into the back of my truck.

"Uh oh, better get Maaco," I laughed, amused in my drunken state. In one quick motion, she grabbed my pistol from the glovebox, my knife from the door pocket, got out, and walked back to the vehicle that hit us. All of this as I clumsily struggled to untangle myself from my seat belt.

Finally freed, I got out.

POP! POP! I saw the fire from the barrel light up his car's interior, then her doing a repeated punching motion. The two shots killed him, the additional stabbing was just overkill.

"Get back in the truck," she said.

"Wait, what just...?"

"GET BACK IN THE FUCKING TRUCK!"

I flinched.

THE END

Nine years later...

It was a cool September morning. Wednesday. The sky was a perfect, clear blue. There was a light breeze that said summer's on its way out, and fall is on its way in.

Karma Lucas stepped outside of a two bedroom apartment and looked up, shocked to see a bird fly into the window of the place she'd just left. It fell to the ground, twitching, flopping around, trying to get up. Its neck was broken. Karma hurried over and picked it up.

"What's wrong, little bird? What happened?" She tried to support its head as she held it close, trying to comfort it. The bird continued to twitch and flutter its little wings.

"Do you need help flying? Do you need Mama to help you fly?" she asked, assuming the role of the bird's parent.

"Here! Fly then!" Karma flung the bird as high up in the air as her muscles allowed, then stepped back and watched it fall right back down to earth, splattering bird blood on the pavement.

"What's wrong with you, dumb bird!' she yelled, "Fly! Fucking fly!" She reached down bare-handed, grabbed the bird, and threw it up in the air again. "FLY!" she screamed.

Splat!

"That's not how birds work, love," Patricia Brown, Karma's best friend, said, coming from the apartment, shutting the door behind her. "Come on, you can't afford to be late again. You're gonna get fired!"

"Ok, lady, I'll see you there," Karma said.

Patricia rubbed her friend's shoulder as they parted and headed to her car at the end of the road. Karma stared down at the dead bird with a tear in her eye.

"Why didn't you fly? I tried to help you," she whispered.

Honk honk

"KARMA! GIRL, LET'S GO!" Patricia yelled from her car as she drove by.

Karma waved, then ran across the street, narrowly missing being run over by an orange Mustang.

Honk! Honk!

"MOVE BITCH!" someone yelled.

"FUCK YOU! LEARN HOW TO DRIVE ASSHOLE!" She yelled back. "332 HJL. 332 HJL." She repeated the license plate number until she got in her car and entered it into the reminder app on her phone. "I got your bitch right here," she mumbled to herself as she did.

Karma took one last look at the apartment building, specifically, the window of the place where she and Patricia had left a man's mutilated body lying on his kitchen's linoleum floor. **-Excerpt from WHAT COMES AROUND The Story of Karma, book 2 of the OVERKILLING THE PAST trilogy**